I0817819

The Year I Made 12 Dresses

...the almost-but-not-quite-true story...

Patricia J. Parsons

Moonlight Press | Toronto

This is a work of fiction. The characters and events in this book are fictitious. Any similarity to real persons, living or dead is coincidental and not intended by the author.

THE YEAR I MADE 12 DRESSES

Cover Illustration: Natalia Lavrinenko via Pixabay

ISBN

978-1-7772431-1-1

For information or permissions:

Visit www.moonlightpresstoronto.com

Or email moonlightpressinfo@gmail.com

This book is for Gwen, Lee, Kerry, Lesley, Kate, Amanda, Maureen and all the other amazing women who I've been privileged to know throughout my life.

December 31

Somewhere between that unwanted – and certainly unneeded – extra glass of champagne and the drunken rendition of a crowd singing Auld Lang Syne at the stroke of midnight, I begin to wonder what the fuss is all about. It happens to me every year.

Somewhere by someone unknown, it's decreed that we should have this wonderful time. We're expected to party until dawn. We must be festive. Perhaps more than anything, it's all that forced joviality that really bums me out. But we all do it, don't we? We smile all evening, then when the ball drops or the clock strikes, we kiss someone we might not otherwise kiss, then we stumble home only to wake up on the first day of a new year wondering where the last day of the old year went. We did it again. And there always seems to be this undercurrent of longing for something to be just a little different this year.

Every year since I finished university, I've woken up on the first of January thinking about something Alfred Lord Tennyson wrote in a play about Robin Hood. I'm not sure why I remember it from an otherwise yawn-inducing required course. But the line stuck with me. "*Hope smiles from the threshold of the year to come, whispering, 'It will be happier.*" Will it? Honestly? Will this year really be happier? Better? More successful?

At some point over the past year, I decided that this upcoming year that will dawn tomorrow *will* be unlike previous years. I know I've said that before, but this year, I already know. It *will be* different. There's always a catch, though, isn't there? Be careful what you wish for, as they say.

You see, my mother died on Christmas Eve. Seriously poor timing, don't you think? So, I've had about a week to get used to being a thirty-two-year-old orphan. I was sad, but given the stuff going on here since then, I've almost gotten over any grief I might otherwise have felt. Mom wasn't even sick, as far as we knew, so it was a bit of a shock to us – by which I mean to me and my older sister, Evelyn. And it's mostly because of Evelyn that I've been so annoyed for the past week that I haven't even had time to feel sad about Mom being gone.

Am I the only person in the world who has a sister from hell? I know I'm supposed to love her – and if push comes to shove, I know I do – but she is so self-righteous and so perfect. She's always right, and she always knows best. It has been this way ever since I can remember. This is possibly the very worst kind of sibling to have in the event of a parent's death. If you have such a sibling, the minute you hear the news of a parent's demise, run. Run as fast as you can in the opposite direction and let that sibling take over. The real problem arises when that sibling keeps saying, "You take the lead. I'm only trying to help." Have you ever heard that old admonition, "Lead, follow or get out of the way"?

I actually said it to Evelyn on Boxing Day when she was rifling through Mom's somewhat disorganized files, advising on everything from the number of death certificates we'd need to how many vases of flowers we'd have to have at the funeral and what kind they should be. "Not lilies," she kept saying. "No lilies. They remind me of death."

Well?

She kept flapping around from one thing to another, brushing off every single idea I offered, then had the audacity to say, "Well, you're in charge. You live closest."

I do live closest, in fact, a great deal closer than she does. *But if I'm supposed to be in charge*, I was thinking, *why is it that you are lording it over everyone?* And by "everyone," I mean me.

So, I finally summoned the courage to say, "Evelyn, for god's sake, do it all yourself, let me help you or get the hell out of my way!" She stopped dead in her tracks and snorted.

“Charlotte Hudson,” she said, hands on hips as if we were once again ten and twelve years old, “you are the most ungrateful sister on the face of the earth. I just lost my mother and this is how you treat me?”

Hello? She just lost *her* mother? What am I? Chopped liver? I lost *my* mother, too. It was so Evelyn.

January

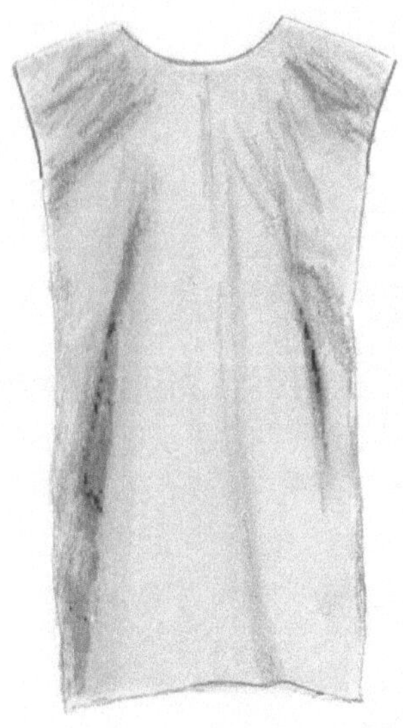

After Mom's funeral, Evelyn and I had what passes for a real talk when it comes to the two of us, perhaps our first since we were pre-teens if pre-teens ever engage in deep(ish) conversation. Everyone had finally left the house where we had hosted the requisite gathering replete with finger sandwiches and tea. Don't get me started on the idiocy of these gatherings. The only thing I wanted to do after the funeral was to hole up with a bowl of popcorn or potato chips, a really good vodka martini and Netflix. I just wanted them all to go away.

All those people I never knew cared so much about Mom. But they came, and they ate. We had to hide the liquor, though, since we, or at least I, had a deep acquaintance with Mom's recent circle of close friends. The only good thing about the whole dismal undertaking was that my oldest friend Summer appeared out of nowhere (we hadn't seen each other in over five years – where does the time go?), lasagna in hand. That's the other thing I cannot figure out about a death in the family: why do the neighbours insist on depositing all manner of casseroles and other reheatable foodstuffs on the grieving family? Have they not suffered enough? Don't they know that potato chips and vodka would be more welcome?

Summer had married Lionel, her high school sweetheart two years before we drifted apart. I always found it awkward to be around someone's husband when all I could think about was that one truly appalling time that I'd had too much to drink and had regretfully slept with Lionel. It was mortifying. These days, if I were a different kind of person, I'd probably be chanting #Metoo, since I couldn't remember agreeing to do anything at all with him. The truth is I would probably not have chosen to be in any room alone with him if I had not imbibed just one too many vodka tonics at one of Summer's many parties. Lionel suffered from serious halitosis back then, so he wasn't high on my list of must-haves, or must-dos.

In any case, I do believe that I am responsible for my own actions, and I did follow him into a dark room, laughing and hiccupping all along the way. That I remember. In my defence, he *is* kind of cute, halitosis notwithstanding, and although he and my best friend had been a thing back in high school, they weren't at that time. A hiatus, I think Summer called it. Anyway, it wasn't my finest moment, but I take my half of the responsibility for it. I put the whole thing behind me, then moved on. A year later, they were back together, and Summer was sporting an eye-popping diamond. Lionel had gone to law school with my sister Evelyn as it turns out and was doing very well in his civil law practice. That's about the time I began to feel a bit awkward around him. Anyway, that's when Summer and I drifted apart. It might also have been related to the fact that Summer had gone to nursing school and had this serious, responsibility-laden job. I, on the other hand, continued to pursue my dream of being a writer (with a side hustle stacking books at the university library). I surrounded myself with other wannabe artist-writers who ate Kraft dinner and drank cheap wine, all the while exchanging horror stories of rejections by agents and publishers. I think they might be what is affectionately called "starving artists," but I didn't always see myself that way, all outward appearances to the contrary.

So, here was Summer after the funeral, giving me a bear hug and telling me how sorry she was when she heard about Mom's death and how Mom had been so young. I guess seventy-three is young to die, but Dad was only sixty-two when he died, so there's that.

Anyway, after the hug, Summer took hold of my hand and put it into her super-large, Louis Vuitton carry-all, where my fingers immediately wrapped around what felt like a vodka bottle. Now we were talking. Or at least drinking. So, it was an hour after everyone – including Summer – had left when Evelyn found me sitting alone in the kitchen with an empty glass on the table in front of me. I had put what remained of the bottle away so I'd stop drinking and potentially avoid a nasty hangover the next morning.

So, the two sisters were finally alone in the house. Mom's house.

I looked up at Evelyn who seemed to be hovering over me. "Where's Michael?"

"On his way to the airport," she said tersely. "He's got a lot on his plate."

Evelyn's husband always had a lot on his plate, as did she. I was slightly surprised she wasn't with him on the way to the airport, but there was a lot on the plate right here, too.

The truth is I was feeling too mellow to care about what I knew was coming: a pompous commentary on my life choices, my prospects and my behaviour, and what we (meaning I) ought to do next. After all, we were sitting smack dab in the middle of the biggest obstacle to the rest of our lives: Mom's rambling, ranch-style house on a charmingly large corner lot with mature trees – at least that's how I pictured a realtor describing it. Truth be told, the ad ought to say "crumbling bungalow in the middle of a garden well past its best-before date." We had harped to Mom for the ten years since Dad had died to sell the house and move to a carefree retirement apartment. She had adamantly refused. I could remember her standing in this very kitchen, hands on her hips, staring us down. "Girls," she had said, "I am not old enough for a retirement apartment. Too many old people." Of course, she was entirely correct. This is how we got here.

Evelyn peered accusingly at my empty glass. "Is there even a drop of liquor in this house? Did Mom stop drinking?" She noisily opened and closed cupboard doors one after the other. "Did you buy any liquor this week?" Evelyn said, eyeing my empty glass again, then continuing to rummage through Mom's kitchen cupboards.

I wasn't thinking about liquor as she hunted her way through the kitchen then repeated her search in the dining room. I was tipsily beginning to think about how much stuff we were going to have to throw out to get the house ready to sell. Up until this moment, I hadn't considered the fact that it was going to be kind of a big job. I was also mildly surprised Evelyn wasn't searching for coffee. I hardly ever saw her when she wasn't clutching a cup of over-priced coffee in her expensive refillable mug. It was her constant companion, it seemed.

"Liquor, Charlie? Are you listening? Is there any wine or booze of some sort? I really could use a drink." She closed a door and turned around. "By the way, you look as if you've already had one. Or two. That glass didn't have water in it, did it? Where are you hiding it?"

I managed to arise from the kitchen table where I had been sitting, being as dignified as I could. I shuffled over to the pantry. I pulled out the now half-empty vodka bottle and a bottle of gin. "There are three bottles of some kind of white wine in the bottom of the vegetable crisper in the fridge," I said, stumbling back to my chair. "I hid them under the wilting lettuce."

"Forget the wine," she said, reaching for the gin bottle. "I see a martini in the making. You don't suppose Mom has any vermouth around here anywhere?"

"She keeps it at the bottom of the china cabinet in the dining room." Since I was the sister who had stayed behind in our home town, I did know a thing or two about Mom and her habits. She had always loved a good, dry martini, and so did her bridge-loving friends, which was the reason I had hidden the liquor before letting them into the house after the funeral. There would have been nothing left by this point.

I watched Evelyn as she expertly mixed her own very dry gin martini. She had managed to find a mixing glass in the china cupboard as I knew she would, then strained it into two martini glasses she found next to Mom's bottles of Ensure, that gross meal supplement drink that older people seem to think they need, in the refrigerator. And to think Mom had insisted she wasn't old? Mom always kept chilled martini glasses in the fridge. You just never knew when you might need one, she used to say.

Evelyn finally put the two glasses on the table then sat down across from me. "Can't find any olives. We'll have to do without." My very meticulous sister then kicked off her very expensive-looking purple suede pumps, plopped her feet on the squeaky red vinyl seat of the empty chair beside her and took a big swig. "Thank god that's over."

I took a sip of my martini and settled in for the expected tongue-lashing. It never came.

~

We sat for a few minutes in blissful silence enjoying Evelyn's very well-crafted, as it turns out, martini.

"What are your plans, little sister?"

Evelyn hadn't called me little sister for a very long time, and it still made me bristle. She is, after all, only two years older than I am – thirty-four as of next month unless I was mistaken. I always thought that she emphasized the "little" part and only because she felt that she had a "big" life while I had a "little" one.

"My plans?" I put my feet up on the only other vacant chair at the old Formica kitchen table. I know what you're thinking. Formica? Red vinyl? Really? Well, Evelyn bought it for Mom and had it delivered three Christmases ago after Mom had reminisced fondly about kitchens from the 1960s. I don't think Evelyn realized that for Mom, it wasn't "mid-century modern" it was just the way it used to be.

"Yes, your plans." Evelyn sipped her drink with a kind of thoughtful expression on her usually sphinx-like face. She was one of those women who always had to defend her facial expression. "RBF," she always told them. Resting bitch face. She always looked like that. I often wondered if that's how she looked even when Michael wanted to…you know…oh, I really don't want to go there.

Before I had a chance to respond, she continued. "You know, Charlie, I'm going to miss Mom."

I bit my tongue. Evelyn had moved away years earlier – a two-hour-by-plane kind of move away and had only seen Mom once or twice a year ever since. I wondered how she could even think this since Mom hadn't been a fixture in her life for fifteen years or so – since she left for university and never returned except on holidays. And for the past seven years, not even on holidays.

Before I had a chance to think of something suitable to say that wouldn't start a squabble, she began to cry. I mean, really cry. Here was my stoic older sister, she of the RBF, sobbing relentlessly while expensive mascara formed black rivulets trickling down her cheeks, and her nose started to stream. I wasn't expecting this. Not even close. It was more than a bit uncomfortable.

I glanced up at the top of the refrigerator and saw the box of tissues that Mom had always kept there. I raised myself as best I could in my semi-inebriated – okay completely inebriated – state and took it down, placing it directly in front of Evelyn. I think she grunted thanks while immediately plucking four tissues out of the box. She began to blow her nose noisily. What could I do except wait for her to settle down? I thought about patting her on the back supportively but quickly nixed that idea. Instead, I sat back down and finished off my drink. One thing you have to give her credit for – Evelyn pours a mean martini. She finally stopped crying.

"God, what must you think?" she said finally, sopping up wet mascara from her cheek. "Here I am bawling my eyes out. I don't suppose you expected that."

"No, Evelyn, I must say that it did take me by surprise a bit. But of course, you did just lose your mother."

I don't think she noticed the slight note of sarcasm that I just could not resist.

When she finally composed herself, she reached for her large, Chanel tote bag that she had stashed under the table and took out a Chanel compact and lipstick. When she had finished her Chanel maquillage as it were, she sat back, took another sip and said brightly, "Now, where were we? Oh, yes, your plans." It was as if the crying jag had never happened.

I was beginning to feel a bit more compassionate toward my cool-as-a-cucumber older sister when she hit me with a zinger – this one I should have seen coming.

"You know that this house has to be cleared out and staged for sale, right? Well, since you don't have a job – "

I started to argue that I did, in fact, have a job at the library – if only twenty hours a week – when she held up her palm in front of my face to silence me and continued.

"... and I do, and you live in a studio flat or share with room-mates or something, I thought that you could move in here and take care of the details. It'll probably only take a month or two."

And there it was. That old saw. Because I'm a writer without a steady nine-to-five in an office, without any real responsibility, I "don't have a job," at least not a real one like Evelyn. She had never been able to get it through her head that writers don't always sit in front of their computers and write. Sometimes they read and do research. Other times they just sit and think, or people watch. Then they might have to go to a yoga class to clear their minds. And there's always the regular meet-and-kvetch over coffee or wine with a "writers' group." Key to success. Of course, success was always just around the corner. I bristled.

"I sort of do have a job, you know, Evelyn." I stood up and went to the sink to get myself a glass of water.

"Charlie, let's get real, shall we? Your job consists of writing the odd magazine article and chasing that dream of being a famous novelist." She drained her martini glass. "By the way, how do you even pay your rent?"

I shrugged. She had a point. My library gig barely covered it, but I didn't want to burden her with the details of my financial tight-rope walk. But I knew I should change the subject as quickly as possible. How I paid my rent was a discussion/argument I did not want to have with Evelyn. But she was on a roll.

"Well," she continued, seeming to relish her trip along the moral high ground that I could see in progress, "if you want to know the truth, I am well aware that Mom's been supplementing your income for years so that you could pursue this starving-writer-in-a-garret life. I, on the other hand, worked my ass off getting admitted to the bar and setting up a law practice where people – actual people – come to me for advice that could have the most dramatic effects on their lives. I have responsibilities."

Oh, not this responsibilities thing again, I thought as she began mixing another round of drinks.

"And I suppose I don't," I said, sitting back down at the table with my full glass of water. I did, however, wonder where there might be another bottle of vodka or gin around the house.

"There is no supposing about it, Charlie. You don't have responsibilities. None. You spend your days focused entirely on yourself. And while we're on the subject, I think it's high time you grew up."

I was so angry, although the truth is, she did have a point. Again. I didn't have any real responsibilities, but I liked it like that. I wasn't cut out to be a ruthless, big-city litigator like she was. Don't get me wrong. I did admire her for the career she was building, but that wasn't the life I wanted. And Evelyn was entirely correct: Mom had always supported my dream of being a writer. Evelyn was achieving her dream. It just wasn't anything like my dream. I had often thought that Mom must have been a closet artist herself despite all evidence to the contrary.

"Anyway," she continued, "I have to fly home tomorrow. I only stayed behind this evening because I knew that you and I had to make some plans. I have to be at a client's discovery the day after, and I'm not quite prepared. I hadn't planned on a funeral in the middle of my client's court case."

I supposed that Mom ought to have made an appointment with Evelyn to schedule her death. But I chose to keep this thought to myself. "Tomorrow?" I said. "You're leaving tomorrow? When were you planning on telling me this?"

"I'm telling you now," she said, checking messages on her phone. Evelyn, the trial lawyer, had arisen in full, leaving the grieving daughter and loving sibling in the dirt. "So, you'll move in and look after everything that needs to be done for the sale? You can text me any time you need advice or corroboration."

What she really meant was permission – permission from her to do what I thought was best. I knew that there was no use arguing with her. She was not going to stay, and I was. But what I was *not* going to do was text her or call her or any other way contact her for permission to do anything. I'd show her. How hard could it be to get a house ready to sell? Not as hard as it would be for me to get *myself* ready for the sale as it turned out.

~

Evelyn left the next day as promised – or threatened. I spent the night in my old bedroom that Mom had left pretty much as it had been when I moved out seven years ago. I had been twenty-five then and had moved home after grad school so that I could save a bit of money before my writing career truly took off.

Dad had died three years earlier, so it was just Mom and me that year. I thought she'd like the company, but it seemed as if she'd moved on, learning to enjoy her own company. That year I often felt like a boarder she merely tolerated. She went out almost every day, presumably to see her friends. I hardly ever saw her. Eventually, Mom told me she thought I'd make more progress with my writing if I had more independence. She offered to supplement my income so that I could pursue my career – and get the hell out of her house. She didn't say those exact words, but that's clearly what she meant. So, I moved into an upstairs flat in an old house a twenty-minute walk away from Mom's house with three other starving artists: an actor, a painter, and a fellow writer.

The two-story house had been a frat house for as long as I could remember: Delta Delta Phi (ΔΔΦ), the symbols for which were still emblazoned above the front door and on the wall leading upstairs to our flat. That was before the fraternity sold it to our current landlord who had made very few upgrades since then. The stairs creaked so that anyone in any of the four flats would always know if someone was coming in. I guess it served as a low-tech security system of sorts.

There were two flats on the lower floor and two on the second floor. Ours, at the top of the stairs toward the back of the house, was the smallest. We did, however, each have a bedroom, although calling mine a bedroom might have been stretching credibility just a bit. My room was so small that I had to suspend shelving from the ceiling to find a place to keep my clothes, and when I pushed my chair back from my miniature desk, the chair always hit the side of the bed. On the bright side, there was a window behind my desk. I could gaze at the trees in the back yard as I sat there mulling over my novel manuscript or a magazine article I was penning.

As I lay in my childhood bedroom that night after Evelyn had decamped to the hotel where she was staying – the house always creeped her out – I had trouble sleeping, but not because I was alone in the house. I rather liked the solitude. No, it was for a very different reason.

I looked up at the ceiling, and for the first time, I noticed that there were dark spots and little cracks. Up until that point in my life, I had never given even a passing thought to whether or not there might be leaks or mould or god knows what in the attic of my parents' house. It just wasn't my problem. But now it was.

Then I wondered if I could leave my novel manuscript for a few weeks until I got this sorted out. Would I even remember where I was when I got back at it? Would I have to do all that research over again, just to get into the swing of things? Who was I kidding? The manuscript was crap. I knew it. Starting over was probably the best idea I'd had in a month. But I did have a magazine article in the hopper. At least, the magazine was considering it.

Then, I started thinking about my room-mates. Should I sub-let my room? My room-mates wouldn't like that, but then I'd only be here for a month, two at the most. I could just keep paying my measly rent. But If I sublet, the rent would be taken paid, and not by me. After the house sold, Evelyn and I would have some money. At least I thought we would. I had no idea whatsoever how much this house was worth and how much tax we'd have to pay after Mom's will made it through probate.

Of course, then there was the issue of the "staging" as Evelyn called it. Did people really do that? Well, that would have to wait. I hadn't been in Mom's basement for years, and I was guessing that there would be a lot of rubbish going out of the house first. And there I was all alone looking after it. The truth was that I was glad Evelyn wasn't here in the house with me.

I must have finally fallen asleep because when I woke up, the sun was shining through the small window of my room and my phone was blinking. It was Evelyn just letting me know that she had made it to the airport and thanks for doing all the stuff and blah blah. So, she was gone. I began immediately to feel a bit lighter.

I threw on an old bathrobe of Mom's that I found hanging on a hook on the back of her bathroom door then made my way down to the kitchen to put on some coffee to assuage my headache. Mom was nothing if not a coffee snob. She had been an early adopter to the capsule coffee rage and had become a Nespresso™ aficionado all the way. She often told me that she was utterly awestruck by George Clooney and his coffee ads. So, I filled the water reservoir with tap water, which would have horrified Mom – she used only filtered water for her coffee – and turned it on. Within minutes I was sitting at the red Formica table (I did mention it was red?) sipping my coffee and scrolling through Instagram posts on my telephone. I knew I was procrastinating. I had a big job ahead of me.

After a breakfast of toast from frozen bread I found at the bottom of the freezer and some organic peanut butter that I had to stir with a butter knife for three minutes before I could get it out without dripping peanut oil all across the counter, I finally took a shower. By then, I was feeling a lot better, so it was on to the basement.

Have you ever seen the basement of one of those mid-century ranch houses? They're like bowling alleys. They seem to go on forever – that is unless the late owner of said bowling alley and her late husband are borderline hoarders. When I arrived at the bottom of the stairs, I gazed along a tidy walkway that led to

Mom's washer and dryer. The problem was that the walls of this little walkway were not walls at all. They were stacks of boxes – boxes of every size and shape. Some were plastic bins, but most were cardboard boxes. Some had evidence of an attempt to keep them organized. I drew this conclusion because some of them were labelled in Mom's unique printing. She always used all-caps. As she told it, she skipped grade two and never learned how to print correctly. Other boxes had no identities at all. In fact, few of them did.

I took one down from the top of the pile, planning to open it to begin the process of deciding what had to stay and what had to go when my eyes happened to gaze beyond the "wall" through the hole I had created. I gasped. It wasn't just these piles forming a hallway of sorts. The entire basement was full from the concrete floor to the unfinished ceiling. Dear god, I would never get through it all.

~

It was January 10 at 9:30 p.m. While the snow whirled outside the windows, I sat in front of the television in what passed for the den, sipping a glass of some kind of wine that I found in Mom's cupboard. I was too tired to be even remotely aware of what was on the screen when Evelyn finally called to check up on me. I had been expecting it to come at some point.

"So, how's it going?" she said. I could hear her take a sip from something that, if I were a betting woman, I would say was probably a dry martini with three olives. It was too late in the day for coffee.

I didn't quite know how to answer that question. I had been thinking about it earlier in the day. How *was* it going indeed?

"Well, it's going," was all I could think of in response.

"When will the house be ready for staging?"

I think I must have snorted some wine up my nose. The next thing I knew, it was dripping down onto my sweatshirt, which was, thankfully, black, so I didn't have to worry about it showing. *Ready for staging*, I was thinking, *I was about ready to call in a demolition unit.*

"Are you still there?" Evelyn was starting to sound a bit whiny. Not a good sign.

"Still here, Evelyn." I wiped my face with a napkin left behind from my dinner, the take-out detritus from which was still scattered on the coffee table. "Frankly, this is going to take a while, and I'm not sure I can get through this by myself. It's a bigger job than I anticipated."

"Don't be ridiculous. I certainly can't take the time to come home and do it for you. And you have nothing else to do."

Why oh why did she have to keep bringing this up? I know she had a "career," and as she saw it, I had a fantasy. It made me mad every time she said it. I was, however, too bone-tired from having spent ten hours out of every day for the past week rifling through box after box of stuff – junk, paraphernalia, trappings of someone else's life. Ephemera. It had started as a bit of a treasure hunt but had quickly deteriorated into a fishing expedition where each fish is even more malodourous than the last one. I had made very little progress that could have, in any circumstance, be described as constructive. She had no idea.

"When was the last time you were in Mom's basement, Evelyn?"

"I haven't the foggiest idea. I suppose it was before Dad died. But what does that have to do with anything anyway?"

"Well, sis, let's just say that we didn't have any idea of the extent of Mom's hoarding tendencies."

"God, you artistic types like to exaggerate," she said, sniffing haughtily.

I was too tired to argue with her and her plethora of prejudices about "artistic types."

"Okay," I said, "let's just say that the whole project is going to take a bit longer than anticipated."

"Well, let me know how it progresses. We have to sell that house at some point, you know."

I knew that. Believe me, I knew that.

~

It was ten days after Evelyn's call that I found it. I was sitting on a small wooden stool with a painted white seat that I had found among the boxes and baskets in the basement. It turned out that the stool was in front of what looked like a small table piled high with yet more boxes. The more I looked at the table, the more I realized that it was a desk-cabinet of some sort – a cabinet I had never seen before. Made of what appeared to me to be teak (perhaps from Mom and Dad's Danish-modern period?), the piece was so dusty it was hard to tell. It had two small drawers on the right and what appeared to be a cabinet door on the left. I tried to open the door, but it was stuck. So, I opened the top drawer to see if it might hold a few clues about the piece.

This is weird stuff, I thought. I pulled out a dusty pair of scissors. I wiped them off on the towel that I kept nearby to dust off objects I came across then looked at them closely, turning them over in my hand. They were large and menacing-looking with a bent handle. Next was a much smaller pair of scissors in the shape of a bird of some sort. I wiped them off too and noted that they were two-toned silver and gold coloured embroidery scissors in the shape of a stork. I suddenly remembered where I had seen them before. My grade seven sewing teacher had a pair on a ribbon pinned to the pocket of the white lab coat she always wore. Miss Davies, I think her name was. God, I hadn't thought of her in years.

I just might keep these, I thought, wiping them until they gleamed. A bit of oil on the hinge, and I'd have a little memento from Mom. The fact that I had never in my life seen her do any embroidery didn't matter. They must have been hers, right? I put them in a plastic bin I also kept with me for objects I thought we ought to keep, or at least objects I thought *I* ought to keep. Evelyn could find her own souvenirs. This was the first such object I had come upon in two whole weeks. Not an auspicious start.

I removed all the boxes from the top of the cabinet and finally managed to open the door. I dragged my old towel over the interior, dislodging a billow of dust. Coughing slightly, I peered into the cabinet. I was a bit startled to find what appeared to be a sewing machine of unknown vintage hanging upside down. It seemed that it could be pulled upright to sit on top of the table.

It was a sewing cabinet. How odd. My mother had never done any sewing – or so I had thought. I wondered whose it was.

I dusted it off and took a photo of it with my phone so I could look it up later. How old was it, and what was it doing in my mother's basement? It said "Pfaff" on the side, and I recognized dials for various kinds of stitches. Miss Davies would have been proud that her worst sewing student remembered what a few sewing machine dials did. Anyway, it would have to wait. I could hear the pizza delivery guy (by now, I knew that his name was Jack) with whom it seemed I was beginning to develop an on-going relationship. He was at the front door. The sewing machine mystery would have to wait.

~

Later that night, as I lay in bed staring up at the ceiling, I again found myself mulling over the mysterious sewing machine. Usually, when I was lying on my bed in the dark these days, I could feel myself becoming overwhelmed by the task that was still almost entirely ahead of me. Although it didn't help with my insomnia, it was a pleasant change to think about something else other than the mountain of boxes

I still had to comb through. I turned over, determined to get to sleep when my phone pinged. It was a text from Evelyn.

"Haven't had an update this week. Things moving along?"

I clicked the phone off. It was an hour later here than there. I decided she could wait until morning.

I was still thinking about the sewing machine the next morning as I filled my coffee cup. I wondered how hard it would be to haul it upstairs. Anyway, I had made the decision that I would try. It seemed like it might be beautiful teak after all – maybe it was the most valuable piece of furniture in the house. In any case, I was going to find out. Before I started that, though, I answered a bunch of text messages.

First to Evelyn: "Moving along. Talk soon." That wouldn't appease her, but she was a busy woman as she reminded me *ad nauseum.* She wouldn't have time to think about me or the house again at least for a few days.

Then there was a text from Summer who had, temporarily as it turned out, resuscitated our relationship via Facebook and text message, wondering how things were going. "Busily cleaning up in Mom's house. Talk soon," I texted. To be honest, I wasn't doing much in the line of cleaning. If I tried to evaluate my progress objectively, it appeared that I had spent the past couple of weeks treading water amongst the flotsam and jetsam of Mom and Dad's life. I had also found stuff that had belonged to Dad that I thought was long gone. After all, it had been ten years for heaven's sake.

Finally, I sent a text to Miriam Mendel, the unofficial leader of the writers' group I usually attended once or twice a month and which I had been avoiding since I wasn't actually, you know, writing. "Busy with Mom's house. Can't wait to get back to the group. Talk soon." This wasn't entirely true. I didn't really want to talk to her soon, and I really *could* wait to get back to the ~~bitching~~ writing sessions, although I didn't want to stop going completely. I found Miriam a bit overbearing, but she did run a tight ship, and the group had been meeting religiously for years. And just as I should have expected, Miriam, whose phone was like an extra appendage, immediately answered.

"Meeting at Joseph's next Wednesday at seven p.m. Expect to see you then. TTFN."

Good god. TTFN? What was she? Thirteen years old? Did thirteen-year-olds even use that one now? Anyway, I couldn't think of a smart rejoinder, so I sent a thumbs-up emoji and made myself a note to remember to go. I must have something in my scribbles that I could take and read. Anyway, Joseph was a real, died-in-the-wool artist-type writer who truly believed that you couldn't be a real writer if you didn't experience drama and angst every day in your life. As a result, everything that happened to him every day from the time he got up in the morning to the time he went to bed every night was one big drama. He made sure that it was. I had often thought that for him, life must be exhausting. For me, his life was endlessly entertaining. I liked to think his angst was my angst, and then I didn't need to have so much drama in my own life. And he had the best-stocked wine cabinet of any member of our group. And, let's be honest: it was the only thing in my current state of existence that even resembled something that could be called a social life. Going wouldn't be so bad.

Once my contact with the outside world had been re-established, I checked in online at the library from which I had taken a few weeks off. I saw my schedule for next week and figured that I'd have no choice but to take the time to actually work outside the house. I couldn't afford to lose the job. Then I set my sights on clearing a path through Mom's basement and up the stairs so I could take a closer look at the sewing machine cabinet.

I spent the rest of the morning moving boxes leading to and around the cabinet. Despite my mounting desire to get the thing upstairs and into the daylight, I thought I probably ought to take a bit of time to look at the contents of some of the boxes as I went. So, with a green garbage bag at the ready, I started to go through some of them.

The first two contained some of Dad's old stuff: mainly tools that he used to tinker with the motorcycle that was supposed to be his retirement project. That didn't work out so well since he died before he had been able to make much progress on restoring the old Harley that he had acquired. Thankfully, it was one thing Mom *had* gotten rid of after Dad's funeral. I think she sold it or gave it away to one of his cycle buddies. I had never understood his interest in it anyway. He was so not a motorcycle kind of guy. Those two boxes were both a toss. They each weighed so much that I had to lift them separately out of the basement and into the large garbage bin I had arranged to have left in the driveway. Their weight possibly explained why Mom had never gotten rid of them. Anyway, the big container in the driveway would be taken away by truck at some point when I was finished. I washed my hands in the mudroom sink on my way back into the house then headed back down the basement stairs.

The next box was somewhat more intriguing. Not nearly as heavy as the last two, it was a large cardboard box labelled "future projects" again in Mom's unique printing. It looked as if it had been there for many years. It made me wonder about what kind of projects my mother was planning to do in the "future" at that point in her life, although truthfully, I didn't know at what point in her life she had written that label. I was beginning to think that I never really knew my own mother.

This box was taped shut by ancient cellophane tape that had yellowed over the years. It was brittle and yielded quickly to the box-cutter I kept in my treasure-hunting arsenal. I opened the flaps to find it filled with envelopes that I immediately recognized from the mists of my distant past – from Miss Davies's classes. They were old sewing patterns, and judging from the drawings, I figured they were probably from the 1970s. They were older than I was.

I put the box on top of the cabinet, which was now cleared off, sat down on the stool and took them out, stacking them neatly in piles of ten each. I had a prickly feeling in the back of my neck as I recognized the pattern company names: Simplicity, Butterick, Style. I remembered them well from Miss Davies's sewing classes. Did I mention that I sucked at sewing?

I picked up the first one on top of pile number one. The drawing on the pattern envelope showed three versions of what I would have called a "hippie" dress. It had a scooped neck that was gathered into a waist belt that wrapped around the body several times. There were two lengths: one that brushed the floor, the other that would have been very much a mini-skirt in those days. I thought it looked as if someone these days might wear it and call it "boho."

The next one was a pattern for a jumpsuit. It was called a "Jiffy" pattern, so I supposed that meant you could make it in a jiffy. I started to giggle. These were sewing patterns for clothes that reflected the style of some forty or fifty years ago, yet they were all the rage these days. I mean, I was a writer who worked part-time in a university library where there was absolutely no need to have any sense of "fashion," but I still seemed to know about it. I guess it's always part of the zeitgeist. Anyway, there were more – scads of them.

There were patterns for what I recognized as granny gown nightdresses, pantsuits, lots of dresses, more boho style tops and skirts, and even hats and bags. I was so confused. None of them seemed to have ever been used. Except for one. I put that one aside and immediately wondered if there might be an online market for these patterns. Were there people out there who actually might be interested in "vintage" sewing patterns? I'd search for that later. Right now, I put them back in the box and proceeded to move the cabinet. It soon became apparent that this cabinet was going nowhere with that sewing machine still in it. I'd have to figure out how to get it out and take the two pieces upstairs separately.

~

I guess my writer colleagues had missed me. While I was eating my lunch of peanut butter on toast (I still didn't have many groceries in), Karl, the one member of the group I had always considered to be the odd-man-out, called me. He is an old-fashioned, telephone-over-texting kind of guy and I liked that about him. Karl was a long-distance truck driver with a wife and three kids. He also had a passion for writing romance novels that had always seemed to me to be out of character – at least if all you saw was his outside. Go figure.

He was over six feet tall, worked out regularly so that he looked like someone you could hire as a bouncer for a rowdy bar downtown. He also sported a series of tattoos on his forearms – and who knew where else.

Karl said that they – or at least *he* was missing seeing me at our writers' group and wondered when I'd be getting back. I told him about my current project, and he was very sympathetic about the loss of my Mom. That was the thing about him. Although he probably wasn't exactly what you might expect a romance writer to look like on the outside, he sure thought and reacted like one. So, I told him about the sewing machine project.

"I can come over and help you get that moved if you like," he said. "I don't have to pick the kids up until 4:30 today." He was on a three-day hiatus before he had to head out on the road again. When he was home, he and his wife shared domestic duties and childcare. Karl made me smile.

“Gosh, Karl, I couldn’t ask you to do that. I’m sure I can manage.”

“Give me a half an hour to clean up from lunch, and I’ll be over with my tools.”

Karl, as always, was true to his word. That’s why by the time the sun was setting on this short winter day, I was sitting in the living room looking at a teak sewing machine cabinet and at a sewing machine that was on a towel on the floor beside it. Karl had removed it from the cabinet for me and suggested I clean it before putting it back, a task which he showed me how to do. It was quite simple. He also gave me some advice on how to restore the teak. I’d make a pilgrimage to my local *Canadian Tire* store in the morning to get the supplies I’d need. In the meantime, I would polish up the machine itself, inside and out. The outside wasn’t going to be a problem, but the inside was an entirely different matter. I was going to need help.

I did an online search for a video or two that might help me figure out how to clean a sewing machine. To my utter astonishment, I was rewarded by thousands of them. Which one to choose? I watched a couple, making it only a few minutes in before realizing that the person on the screen was either hopelessly confusing or had a whiny voice I could not bear to listen to. Just as I was beginning to despair, I happened upon a channel called "Whispering to Fabric with Grace." It sounded a bit new-age spiritual, but what did I have to lose by watching one or two?

It turned out that "Grace" was a woman who seemed to know her way around the outsides and insides of a sewing machine. She could clearly explain and demonstrate exactly what I wanted to do. With a glass of wine by my side and my iPad propped on the table in front of me, I was following the instructions from her video. With her voice in my ear, I carefully removed pieces of the machine, cleaned and oiled them with a few drops of oil I'd found in a bottle in a drawer of the cabinet. According to Grace, sewing machine oil was very specific and using any other kind would result in nothing short of a disaster. Who was I to argue? I then screwed them all back together.

When I had finished that job, I sat down to watch more of Grace's videos. Some kind of sewing whisperer, Grace and her *YouTube* channel had some 52,000 subscribers. 52,000! Who knew there could possibly be that many people in the world who were sewing things with a sewing machine if they didn't work in some kind of a sweatshop in Sri Lanka and were forced to do it to pay for food? Anyway, Grace's voice was mesmerizing, and her videos fascinatingly well-produced. By the time I finally looked away, it was well after midnight. I was surprised to find that I had watched twenty videos! I was beginning to formulate an idea.

~

It was getting close to the end of January. As I looked around the house, it seemed as if I still hadn't made much progress on clearing it out, but I was feeling a bit clearer in my own head. In fact, I was feeling very pleased with myself. I had been able to clean and oil the teak cabinet as best I could, given its age, then I placed it under a window in the den and replaced the sewing machine in it. As I stood in front of it wondering how much someone might pay for a refinished, mid-century-modern teak sewing machine cabinet with a usable sewing machine (at least I thought it was usable – I hadn't dared to plug it in yet), it struck me like a bolt of lightning from on high: it was now mine. I would keep it. I would learn to sew. Strike that: I would teach myself to sew.

When Evelyn texted me later that evening, I was knee-deep in sewing patterns from Mom's boxes from which I was making copious notes. I had my iPad propped up again with my sewing companion Grace on the screen and was madly revisiting the videos I had watched mindlessly the week before. I ignored the text chime until it chimed twice more then I had to look.

"How goes the clean-up?" said the first.

"Are we ready to sell?" said the second.

"Where the f**k are you!" said the third.

I figured I had to answer.

"Still working hard at it," I texted back, feeling only slightly guilty because, at this rate, it was going to take me another two months to finish. In that moment, I realized I didn't care.

"Flying in. See you next Friday. We can assess together."

Shit! She was actually coming. And she wanted to "assess."

"No need. I can handle it." I was hoping she might be dissuaded from spending the money on an airline ticket – and a hotel.

"Already booked. My flight arrives at nine p.m. Renting a car. Staying with you. Make my bed. Please."

Oh. My. God. She was coming *and* staying with me in the house. I guess finding the house creepy was something she had gotten over. I thought I might throw up. But how can you feel this way about your sister? It comes with the territory if you've had to put up with your sister's imperious attitude since you were eight years old. Well, there was nothing whatsoever I could do about it except possibly go into a frenzy of cleaning for the next few days so that it at least looked as if I had been doing something. Yeah, sure – as if I would do that!

Evelyn's unwelcome upcoming visit notwithstanding, after binge-watching some of Grace's hundreds of videos, I had decided that I was going to sew something. I was hoping I could remember a thing or two about sewing seams from those old classes back in junior high. I found a box filled with old lengths of material – a stash I think the online sewing people were now calling it. Yes, Mom's stash. It consisted of one and two-metre lengths of what appeared to me to be cottons. They were actually kind of ugly, all chintz and flowers and wild colours. I wondered what Mom had been thinking when she bought them, assuming she was the one who did. But as I thought about it more, it occurred to me that they had probably been meant to make up some of those hippie dresses in the patterns I had found, although they weren't even remotely her style. It wasn't much wonder Mom had never made them. Anyway, they would make terrific pieces for sewing practice. So, with the thread I had found in yet another box – there must have been a hundred spools – I popped Grace's video on basic sewing up on my iPad, filled a bobbin with thread all by myself (following her instructions) and threaded the machine. This is the short version. I had to try four times to get the thread to go through all the little hooks and washers as per the online instructions and found myself with thread wound around my fingers at least twice. I was finally ready. I plugged it in, took a deep breath and pressed my foot on the pedal.

What a rush! I was immediately back in my junior high school sewing classroom. I could picture Miss Davies standing in front of us with her hands clasped as if in prayer while we, twelve young ladies (I use the word loosely) and one young man (the only one among who seemed to be acutely interested in the skills at hand,) heads down, motored our way along a seam. Although it has to be said that I felt a lot better about it now than I did then. I was sewing classes in those days because Mom suggested it to me for some unknown reason, and it fit in my schedule, but I had little interest in sewing or fashion or style. That much was clear to anyone who saw me in those days. I was in my grunge period. But today was different. This was a kind of a rush. Today I was channelling a couturier's seamstress. Today I was learning to create! But to create something, I was going to need some fabric. Those pieces of flowered stuff were not going to cut it, though. And what was I going to create? I would design and sew a dress. Yes, that's what I'd do. How hard could it be?

~

My writers' group meeting was upon me. I decided to rejoin society, as it were, and appear. Stacking books in the library didn't require much if any, human contact, and I loved it. I didn't have much to share with the group in the way of new writing, but I had managed to find a file that I'd been working on last summer, edited it a bit and printed out a copy to read. We all had to do that before we could eat anything, and I did want to eat – and drink. Although drinking before reading was both acceptable and encouraged. It was sometimes even necessary.

Joseph threw his arms around me the minute I walked through the door. Miriam was already there, as was Karl who waved from the other side of the living room. The only one missing was Wendy, who was always late. A frazzled thirty-something mother of three little children, Wendy wrote children's books and was in perpetual motion. She'd probably be along any time now.

I took off my coat and hung it on a hook behind Joseph's door. When I turned around, the three of them were staring at me.

Joseph cleared his throat. "You look...nice...this evening," he said, then immediately fled to the kitchen presumably to bring out another bottle of wine.

"Good to see you back," Karl said.

Miriam cocked her head to the side. "You look different."

I smiled and smoothed my dress. "I'm wearing a new dress."

"Is that what you call it?" Joseph had returned from the kitchen. I surmised that his lowered voice was so that I might not be able to hear him.

"What do you mean? I made it myself," I said, turning so that they could get the full effect. I had hoped that it might swish or swirl a bit. The fabric, however, stayed stubbornly stiff.

Karl said nothing. Joseph, the most dapper among this group of non-dapper-like writers, stood in front of me. "How long have we known each other, Charlie?"

I thought for a moment. "About seven or eight years, I suppose."

"Yes," he said, "so that means that I can probably tell you the truth."

I nodded, still smiling.

"You look as if you're wearing a shower curtain." He immediately turned away to pour a glass of wine, which he then offered to me. "Wine?"

Miriam was still staring. "Well, I think it's artistic," she said finally.

Oh god. If Miriam liked my outfit, then Joseph was probably right. She was partial to flamboyant mu-mu's, capes and flowing scarves of every type imaginable. This evening she was sporting a purple cape-like top with matching bauble earrings as big as robins' eggs.

"Actually," I said, turning to Joseph, "it *is* a shower curtain if you must know. I *repurposed* it." Who could argue with the notion of repurposing – it was so "green."

I had made a pilgrimage to a thrift store where their selection of shower curtains was nothing short of amazing. Truthfully, many of them were downright hideous, but this one had caught my eye with its muted blue and red horizontal stripes. And who could argue with the price tag? It was two dollars. I realized that I could design a simple dress with a hole in the top for the head and two holes at the sides for arms. I could practice using the sewing machine by sewing up those seams under the arms. I could even curve the neckline. This was my thinking. Dead simple, and on-trend, you know? I was wearing a black turtleneck and tights under it. I figured I looked the very picture of an artist. Why, then, was I feeling a tad defensive about my sartorial choice? Damn it, I was an artist, and now I was a me-made fashionista. I had recently learned the word "me-made" from the online sewing communities I had joined. I had joined about thirteen by that point. And I had Grace on *YouTube* in my corner as well.

Finally, everyone calmed down. When Wendy arrived, she was in such a state about one thing or another she didn't have time to notice my dress which was fetchingly spread around me on the sofa where I was sipping wine and munching on potato chips. I kind of enjoyed being back with this wacky group of writers, their distaste for my clothing choices notwithstanding, of course.

~

The next Friday was the last day of January. It was the end of the first month of the great house cleaning project. I was swishing around the kitchen in my new me-made dress, this time with a red, long-sleeved T-shirt under it. Evelyn walked through the door just before ten that evening, dropped her overnight bag on a chair in the kitchen and poured herself a glass of vodka from the bottle I had already placed on the table – I had recently discovered Tito's handmade vodka. She took a sip then turned to greet me.

"What the actual f**k are you wearing?"

Not even a hello, how are you. These were her first words to me, her dear, hard-working sister. Oh, this was going to be a terrifically warm and fuzzy visit. I could feel it in my bones.

February

I looked at my dear sister and thought, *well, I suppose it's a valid question under the circumstances.*

I smoothed my hands down the front of what I had come to regard as something of a shield from the real world. The shielding thing wasn't working so well against my one and only sibling.

There she was, standing in front of me, her perfectly bobbed hair perfectly in place, her outfit perfectly coordinated, no detail left to chance. She was wearing a slightly severe – at least in my newly fashion-conscious opinion – black suit. The pants were slim cut and ended just above her ankles. The jacket had no lapels giving the impression of being very sleek. Under it, she seemed to be wearing a black T-shirt. I do realize that black is the best colour to wear on planes, but she looked a bit like a crow, and I could see that she was about to caw at me.

Evelyn always reminded me of Anna Wintour, the editor of *Vogue* magazine, with the perfect bangs and bob and professional, no-nonsense, don't-mess-with-me wardrobe. Sometimes her personality reminded me of AW, too, or at least how she was portrayed in that old movie *The Devil Wears Prada*. It was always said that the devil in that movie in the person of the magazine editor was based on Anna Wintour. Anyway, my outfit stood in stark contrast.

"I've started sewing," I said as I reached for a glass and the vodka.

"Sewing? Since when have you been interested in sewing?" She came closer to me, reaching out to touch the fabric. Her hand retracted instantly as if it might have touched poison. "Is that...a shower curtain?"

"Yes," I said brightly, sipping my drink. "I got it at a thrift store."

She withdrew her hand so fast it was as if she had burned herself. "Good lord, Charlie. It might have bed bugs or worse."

What's worse than bed bugs? I thought as I swirled the vodka and ice around in the glass.

"I checked it before I brought it home. It's fine. Maybe the fit isn't so perfect..." I trailed off thinking about how it fit like a bag, but it covered everything, and more importantly, protected me – kind of the way a shower curtain protects the bathroom from getting wet. I liked that.

"The fit? You have to be joking. It doesn't have any fit whatsoever. How in the world did you get an idea like this to start making your own clothes? It's bad enough what you wear on a regular basis." She clapped a hand over her mouth as if she had not meant to say that.

Although we had never actually had a direct discussion before about my wardrobe, I had always felt Evelyn took a dim view of the ripped jeans and drapey jersey T-shirts that had become my everyday wardrobe. I liked clothes, but my lifestyle didn't need fashion. Writers don't need to dress up. Besides, ripped jeans were actually in style these days. I just sniffed and decided not to engage at this time. In any event, I wanted to change the subject, since I wasn't yet ready to share with her my discovery of Mom's old sewing machine, and I could feel her question about how I managed to sew something about to emerge from her pursed lips.

Given that she hadn't mentioned anything about an old sewing machine, I concluded that she hadn't known any more about Mom's sewing endeavours – if that's what they were – than I did. I don't understand why, but that actually made me feel a little better as if I might have edged just slightly closer to Mom than my older sister. In any case, I had hidden the sewing machine in its cabinet and pushed it into a closet I was confident she would never get to this weekend. I was right about that.

To say that the sisterly visit didn't go well would be a profound understatement. Evelyn was livid. What was she livid about? You name it, and she was furious about it.

Every step she took that weekend was cause for further outrage in my sister's mind. The kitchen wasn't pristine. True. The dining room was still exactly like it had been when Mom died. True. The living room was dusty. True. It was all true. So, on Saturday morning, I took her by the hand and led her down the stairs into the basement.

When her foot reached that last step, she grabbed onto the railing as if to steady herself. It was one of those moments where you wished you had a phone in your hand to capture her face. Damn, I had left mine on the kitchen table. Instagram would have loved it. Her eyes widened as she clapped a hand over her mouth again.

"What the actual f**k is this?"

I wondered briefly about the origin of what appeared to be my sister's new favourite phrase and when she had developed such a potty mouth, but that was for another time. I wanted her to get the full effect of the state of the house. That started with the basement. I figured that if she saw it for herself, she might consider the wisdom of rolling up her very pristine Brooks Brothers sleeves and helping – or at least she might consider getting off my back about the continuing mess.

It was clear that neither of us had been fully aware of our mother's proclivities. It was also clear that this had been going on for a very long time. Mom, it seemed, had had all the makings of a secret hoarder – one of those people whose public spaces where they entertain family and friends look reasonable, even obsessively perfect. That's all a smokescreen for the reality of what lies beneath, literally and figuratively. The added horror of it was the realization that Dad had probably aided and abetted her unless, of course, he had been the hoarder, and that seemed highly unlikely.

At that moment, I thought it prudent to let my sister in on one essential piece of information. That she could see a pathway between the boxes and any light at all from the basement windows was a testament to the fact that I had not been lazing around the house. I had been working my tail off. What lay before her *was* progress.

Well, if I thought that my perfect sister was going to get her hands dirty and help me sort through more than a few boxes, I was mistaken. To her credit, though, she did start by saying, "Well, then, let's get at it, shall we?"

And so, we did. That lasted through three boxes, all of which contained nothing but junk that had to be tossed. Evelyn's reaction was typical.

"Charlie, let's just get someone to come and empty the basement. I can find a company to haul all of this away."

"Without checking for things? Without going through everything?"

"What things?" she said, lifting yet another dusty cookbook from the open box in front of her.

We had found at least fifty cookbooks at this point, and I wanted to look in every single one of them to be sure that I wasn't missing a treasured recipe even though I wasn't much of a cook. I had begun to feel that neither of us had truly known our mother. I was afraid that tossing without looking would leave us in the dark for the rest of our lives. Evelyn didn't seem to care one bit. As far as I could tell, she didn't have a nostalgic bone in her body. She just wanted to get it done. She was not the one who had already discovered a treasure in the form of that sewing machine. I stood my ground.

"Evelyn, I'll do it."

"Do what? Go through every one of these boxes?" She waved her hand across the basement.

She did have a point. It would take weeks, maybe even months.

"It will take you weeks. Maybe even months," she said.

Yup. And at that moment, I realized that I was prepared to do it for as long as it took.

By four p.m. that afternoon, despite working through and taking only a half hour for lunch – a glass of wine and toast (we are, after all, not two cat ladies given to eating tea and toast) – we had made very little progress. I would open a box and start taking things out while Evelyn sat there, tapping on her phone and looking up once in a while to see what was emerging. Finally, she stood up.

"I'm going to the pub for a drink and a bite to eat. You coming?"

Ooh, I thought. *A pub dinner instead of take-out.* I was in.

After a drink and a pub dinner of locally-sourced, organically produced fish and chips (Evelyn never let anything un-organic pass her lips other than vodka or gin), she wiped her mouth and put her napkin down. "Okay, Charlie, if you want to go through everything – if you have the *time* to do it – and it means that much to you, go for it. There are only a couple of things I want anyway."

I was all ears. At this point, I had concluded that she thought everything from our childhood was dusty and dirty and didn't fit with her view of herself these days. However, it seemed that Evelyn had long coveted Mom's collection of cranberry glass. When we were kids, Mom had explained to us that these rose-coloured pieces had a long and storied history, a fact that seemed to make them even more valuable in her mind. It's not that they were valuable in monetary terms, rather they had significance for her. There were wine glasses, water goblets and a few genuinely hideous free-form ashtrays and vases with ruffled edges. I was astonished to hear that Evelyn had always liked them. To my untrained design eye, they didn't seem even remotely complimentary to the minimalistic urban style that she and Michael cultivated in their downtown condo. The things you don't know about your siblings! Believe me, I had no use for those objects and told her that I'd even pack them up so she could either take them with her the next time she came, or I'd courier them to her. The other things she wanted were a bit more contentious.

Mom had a collection of Bakelite jewelry. Bakelite is a plastic material that was first used to create jewelry and other objects like purses in the 1920s and 1930s. Mom had been collecting it for a long time before either of us was even born, which isn't difficult to imagine since she was thirty-eight when Evelyn was born and forty when I was born – quite old in her day. Her collection might even be worth something these days. Both Evelyn and I had loved it since the days when Mom would let her two little girls try on bangles and necklaces and carry around her Bakelite purses. I wanted it, too.

We agreed that on her next visit, we would lay all the pieces out and divide them up between us.

The next morning, Evelyn flew home, and I again felt a lightness settle over me.

Later that day, I took the sewing machine out of the closet and arranged it under the window in the dining room again. I sat down in front of it on the little stool and stared at it as if it might tell me what I should do next. *I should give it a name*, I thought. But what to name it?

I stared at it a bit longer, willing a name to emanate from its pulleys and pistons and thread carriers. Suddenly it came to me: Charlie junior. Junior for short. So, I vowed to get to know Junior better. I knew that I ought to tackle a few more boxes in the basement, and I'd get to that, but there were other things I wanted to do first.

I went back upstairs and pulled my new "dress" out of the closet. *I can do better*, I thought. I stood in front of Mom's full-length mirror and held it up in front of me. I realized that it was, in fact, really nothing more than a bag. And it was also probably quite hideous – in conventional terms. And the fact that Miriam had actually liked it made it even more suspect as a real piece of clothing.

As I stood there, I began to wonder, though, why I even cared when I clearly had more important or at least more pressing things to do. I never liked sewing when I took it in junior high school. As I mentioned, I took it only because Mom suggested it to me, and it fit into my class schedule. As I stood there in front of the mirror, I began to wonder why Mom did that. I had never asked her.

She knew I had never shown the slightest bit of interest in sewing or style or even clothes for that matter. I was a free spirit artist. I not only considered myself to be a writer even then, penning short stories full of teenage angst (I shuddered now to even think about them), but I also fancied myself a sort of visual artist. I had a set of charcoals and drawing pencils and coil-bound pads of sketching paper stuffed into the back of a desk drawer. I was abysmal in that department, but I never let that stop my free-flowing dreams of artistic triumph. I felt important when I was sketching or writing. It felt like the only time I wasn't in the shadow of my academically brilliant older sister. I stared at myself in the mirror for a bit longer and considered trashing it but instead put the "dress" on a hanger and placed it in the closet. I *could* do better.

I went downstairs and opened up the box of patterns I had found. These were real patterns for real clothes. The front of each envelope had a drawing that told me so. I pulled out a few that looked simple then, deciding that I had learned enough from Miss Davies all those years ago, figured that I could probably manage an uncomplicated one. What could be less complicated than a simple, round-necked sheath dress? No sleeves to worry about and only a few straight seams. What could possibly go wrong? Anyway, it was clear that I'd be needing fabric. Maybe not a shower curtain this time?

~

I live in a small city on the Atlantic coast. I have lived here all my life. It has quaint historic buildings on the waterfront, several streets of pubs, restaurants and clubs, hordes of tourists in the summer, a few boutique-type shops and lots of office buildings. No one lives downtown, though. They live in the suburbs and shop at sprawling suburban malls with chain stores. Even though they don't live downtown, people here love their little city. They love it so much that every time someone has an idea to build something new, like an office building or a condo, regardless of its aesthetic or functional value, there is an inevitable outcry of protest. The protesters argue for maintaining the heritage, the tradition, frankly often the old and decrepit. That's one of the reasons that Evelyn left and never came back. She loves new and tidy and sparkly, and urban. As for me, well, I like new and tidy, but I also kind of like the old and decrepit if I'm totally honest. Anyway, I like the downtown just the way it is. I guess I do like things to stay the same. I'm not a suburban-mall kind of girl. So, when faced with the need to procure something other than a shower curtain or table cloth at a thrift shop, I bristled at the idea that I'd have to go to some kind of chain-store fabric outlet to find something suitable for my new project. What, then, was the alternative?

Years earlier, when I had been in those sewing classes, I had spent some quality time browsing through two or three tiny fabric stores that lived in odd places on small side streets. One of them was between a pizza joint and a tattoo parlour. If you didn't really know where you were going, you'd probably miss the door, potentially ending up with a tattoo of a sewing machine on your forearm instead of a new sewing machine. If you did happen upon the right door, once inside, you had to make your way up a set of dilapidated stairs. (It was one of those heritage buildings that the building-huggers work so hard to keep from falling prey to developers, but fail to keep in fire-safe condition.) After creaking your way to the top, you emerged in an attic space jammed to the actual rafters with bolts of fabrics. The visual assault was dizzying, as I recalled.

Summer, who was also taking sewing classes with me, and I would poke around looking for material for school projects. Still, since we didn't really see ourselves as "seamstresses," we had also been seized by the notion that we might become fabric artists. You know what I mean: we'd cut out bits of fabric and stick them on poster board or something. That idea never really fully materialized. I wondered if that store still existed. Instead of checking online (I figured that they weren't the type of store to be online – besides, I couldn't remember what they were called), I decided to wander downtown and see for myself. Before I left, I stuffed a few patterns in my backpack so I'd have something to refer to if I found some fabric.

Dropping another green garbage bag in the bin in the driveway on my way out, I pulled my scarf tight around my neck to keep out the February wind, swung my backpack over my shoulder and headed to the bus stop. It was way too cold to walk all the way downtown.

I hadn't been on a local bus in a while. When you essentially work in your pyjamas almost every day and are within walking distance of your part-time library job, there's not much need for the commute downtown. Anyway, at that time in the middle of the morning, there weren't very many people on the bus. I found myself wondering about each of their stories. A young woman was sitting across from me, her head down staring into a cell phone. I could see that she'd been crying and wondered what had happened to her.

In front of her was an older man in a threadbare coat that looked as if it might have been expensive in its day. He had a full head of silver hair and a straight back that belied his age. I wondered what his story was. I was beginning to think I should get out more often. Maybe I would shake my writer's block. Oh, yes, I had writer's block. Why on earth would I be spending my days rummaging through Mom's stuff and taking a flight of fancy on making a piece of clothing? Simple avoidance.

I got off the bus a block short of where I remembered the shop had been. As I looked toward the space, I was disappointed. All I could see was the canopy of what appeared to be some kind of upscale restaurant. Wow! Had this part of the downtown ever changed! So, where to now?

I was trying to remember where the other fabric shops had been all those years ago. As I slowly made my way up the block, I noticed up ahead a huge yellow canopy over the sidewalk under which there were what I can only describe as barrels containing tube-like bolts of fabric. I was surprised to see merchandise displayed outdoors. After all, it was February, but at least fabric wouldn't freeze even if the customers did. As I approached the barrels, I looked up at the red lettering on the canopy. It said *Sew Fine Things*.

The shop was what I'd call slightly non-prepossessing. The windows were hazy with grime, and the door looked as if it might fall off its hinges upon the next person opening it. But it seemed to be the only game in town at that moment in my life, so I gingerly approached it, glancing at the myriad cotton prints and neon-coloured tulle fabrics that spilled out of the barrels as I reached for the door. As I stepped out of the February sunshine and over the threshold, I found myself immediately in a different world.

As my eyes adjusted to the dimmer light (those grimy windows and the canopy didn't let in much natural light), I was momentarily overtaken by the tableau in front of me. As far as the eye could see – which wasn't that far since the store wasn't massive – bolts of fabric lined the narrow aisles from floor to ceiling. It was a riot of colour and texture, the like of which I had never experienced in my life. I felt a bit like what I had always thought Alice in Wonderland must have felt as she encountered that hookah-smoking caterpillar. I wasn't at all sure I liked what I was seeing, but I was captivated by it, and it drew me in as if by some force of nature.

I navigated my way past more barrels of what I now saw to be discounted fabric bolts and a large wooden chest holding little bundles of fabric done up with elastic bands: "remnants" was what the sign above it said. Leftover bits, maybe? There was a large, old-fashioned cash register on top of a long counter that I presumed was where the fabric was measured and cut. I did, however, seem to be alone in the shop. It was eerily quiet.

I began to make my way down one aisle and up the next, stepping over more bolts of fabric that were leaning against the shelving because there appeared to be no more room for them. I heard a disembodied voice.

"Let me know if you need any help," it said.

I was so startled I didn't immediately respond. I wasn't sure what startled me most: the fact that I wasn't alone in the shop, or that the voice was a deep baritone with just a hint of an exotic foreign accent. Finally, I found my voice. "Sure, thanks," was all I could manage.

Since I had no idea whatsoever what I was looking for, I couldn't begin to know what kind of help to ask for. And what about that deep voice? I guess I expected a fabric store clerk to sound like Miss Davies: slightly squeaky but enthusiastic as I recalled.

I moved slowly down each aisle, lightly touching various fabrics as I went. Some felt cool to the touch, some warm. Some were nubby, almost gritty, while others were as smooth as I figured real silk would be. Needless to say, I didn't have much experience with various fabrics beyond reading the care labels in my clothes, most of which were made in Sri Lanka or Vietnam, presumably in some kind of sweatshop. The thought always made me slightly queasy, but my budget didn't permit me to be that fussy. And I wasn't much into re-using clothes cast off by others to the thrift shops – notwithstanding my foray into repurposed shower curtains. I remembered that Miss Davies used to tell us that we could have beautiful clothing at a fraction of the cost if we would learn to sew them ourselves. Summer and I never did believe her. But now, standing here amid all this fabric, I wondered if she might not be right. I hadn't thought of that in years.

I began looking more closely at the labels: cotton – I recognized that one – but I wasn't at all sure I knew what "cupro" was. And Tencel? That rang a dim bell somewhere in my mind. I sighed. This was going to be harder than I thought.

I turned the corner and was stopped in my tracks as I looked up from the bolt of fabric I was caressing to find myself nose to knee with what appeared at first glance to be a giant of a man. A second glance told me he was standing on a small ladder, but he was, without a doubt, a tall man.

"Sorry to startle you," he said in that baritone with a slight accent. He stepped down from the ladder where he had been arranging bolts of fabric.

He wasn't a giant, but he was a tall, muscular man with dark cropped hair and skin the colour of *café au lait.* He had a hint of a dark beard with flecks of grey, although he appeared to be mid-thirtyish if I guessed correctly – perhaps only a year or three older than I was. He also wore dark-rimmed glasses that gave him an air of gravitas for someone so young. For some reason, the strength of his presence made me move back slightly as if it might be a good idea to give him more space. I wasn't *at all* sure if I ought to be alone in a small, quiet shop with this man. Then he smiled.

He smiled not with his lips so much as with his eyes. They seemed to glow softly as he wiped his hands on a piece of paper towel.

"Hi there," he said, extending his hand, "I'm Al. I don't think I've ever seen you in the shop before."

"Hello," I said, hesitantly shaking his outstretched hand. I was immediately struck by the firmness, yet gentleness of his handshake. "Nice to meet you." I hesitated for a moment. "I'm Charlie."

He laughed softly. "Charlie, is it? Well, Charlie, what can I help you with today?"

"Well," I said, overcoming an unaccustomed hesitation, "I'm looking for some fabric, and I really don't know much about it. Is there someone around who could help?"

"I can help you."

"Um, I'm kind of hoping I can talk to someone who knows how to sew. I'm kind of a novice."

He crossed his arms and cocked his head slightly to the right. I could see his biceps bulging under the long sleeves of his T-shirt.

"What makes you think that I can't help you with that?"

I didn't know what to say. I was thinking that he didn't look like someone who would know how to sew, but I didn't think that it was appropriate to say that. After all, who was I to judge what people who sewed looked like these days? Maybe it was "a thing" and I didn't even know that. And I remembered the one, lone boy in my sewing class all those years ago.

"I don't look like your old sewing teacher, do I?"

How did he know that I was thinking that? The very thought of Miss Davies standing here beside "Al" actually made me giggle slightly.

"Ever heard of a guy called Earl Nightingale?" he said.

I shook my head, although it did sound familiar. "Does he sew?"

Al laughed and shook his head, no. "Probably not important, but he had a lot of wise things to say in his life. He once said, '*When you judge others, you do not define them, you define yourself.*'"

I was once again startled by Al. I never expected someone like him… Good lord, he was right. I *was* pre-judging him because he didn't look like Miss Davies.

"Gosh, I'm sorry. I didn't mean…"

He uncrossed his arms and smiled again. "No problem. But I really *can* help you. Try me."

~

I was in the shop for two hours. Several people, all of whom seemed to know Al quite well, came and went buying this piece of fabric or that cone of thread. While he waited on them, I touched the texture of fabrics, smelled the fabric-shop aromas, listened to the cash register pinging and gazed along the narrow aisles with their mesmerizing array of colours. There were so many shades and tints and patterns. It was so much to take in that I felt as if my head might explode. In between customers, Al would come over to tell me about the bolt of fabric I was drooling on.

"That one's a dobby weave," he said, running his hand over the slightly ribbed texture of the striped fabric that had caught my eye.

"Dobby?"

"Yeah, if you look closely, you can see tiny geometric patterns woven into the fabric. This one's cotton. Do you like it?"

I did and told him so.

"What're you planning to make?"

That was a more difficult question to answer. "I'm not sure. I thought maybe a dress." I ran my hand over the fabric feeling its texture.

"What style?"

Gee, this was going to be difficult. "Not really sure."

"Do you have a pattern?"

So, I told him about Mom's box. Then I told him about finding the sewing machine and fixing it up and being possessed with this idea that I would sew a few things.

"Okay, Charlie, let me get this straight. You want to make a dress, but you don't have any idea what it will look like, what it should be made of or of how to put it together."

"Well, I found a lot of online videos that teach sewing. And I did take sewing classes when I was in junior high."

"Would you mind a suggestion?"

"Fire away."

Al suggested that I start with a simple shift-dress pattern. I hadn't shared with him my January project, aka the shower curtain dress. I rummaged in my backpack and pulled out one of Mom's old but never-used patterns.

"Is that one of the patterns you found in your Mom's basement?" he said, taking it from me and immediately turning it over to read the back of the envelope. "Are there more like this?"

"Oh, yes. I found scads." I said, calculating for a moment. "I suppose there are at least a hundred. Maybe more."

His eyes widened as he whistled softly. "Are they uncut like this one?" I must have looked puzzled. "Have they been used?"

"Not as far as I can tell," I said, taking another one out of my bag. "Actually, I've only found one that looks as if it's been used."

"These are extraordinary," he said, placing them side-by-side on the cutting table. "This one," he said, pointing to the second one. "You should start with this one. It's from the 1970s, but I think it will work today. And I have just the fabric for you."

The envelope said it was a "sew and go" kind of project. It was also called "the flare jumper." It sounded good to me.

~

As the door to *Sew Fine Things* closed behind me an hour later, I stepped back out into the sunlight and the cold. The street was just as I had left it, but somehow it wasn't the same. I wasn't the same. What had just happened?

I felt as if I had emerged from another world – a world where even in the dimmed light, the colours were brighter, the smells were more agreeable, the sounds more muted and comforting. I took a deep breath of the cold air and shifted my plastic bag under my arm. The bag contained a piece of navy-blue fine wale corduroy, a fabric that I would never have considered wearing in a million years – before today – and two spools of matching thread. Al had suggested that I make a jumper that needed a zipper down the back. I assured him that trying to sew a zipper might be a bridge too far at this point, so we agreed the almost-tent-like jumper pattern probably didn't need one anyway. That's when I agreed to the corduroy, which he said would be easy to work with. And I was happy with another tent, this time a tent that might actually fit me better. So that's what was in the bag. But I somehow felt it wasn't all.

As I sat on the bus on the way home, I didn't notice anyone around me this time. I had too much to think about. I had a growing feeling that there was *much* more in the bag than fabric and thread. Like the piece of fabric itself, whatever was hiding there was also unformed, yet to find its final shape. But it was as real to me as the spool of thread I could feel under the plastic of the bag. And I remembered Al's admonition not to pre-judge.

~

On February 28, I finished the last stitch in the hem of my new jumper and called the junk collectors to take away the first of what promised to be at least three bins full of discarded items from Mom's basement. It was a good day. And as I sat on the bottom step of the basement stairs looking at what still lay ahead, I didn't have that same sense of dread that had enveloped me on that first trip down here after Mom's funeral. Although, to be honest, there were still hundreds of boxes – or so it seemed – staring at me as I gazed around the dimly-lit space. The basement still had that musty concrete smell that had put me off when the task began. But I was thinking about something Al had said when I whined that I might never get the jumper finished at the rate I was likely to learn to sew again. (It turns out I was wrong about my sewing speed.) He quoted Confucius, who apparently said, "*It doesn't matter how slow you go as long as you do not stop.*" My house-clear-out job was going slowly, but I knew I'd get there. I wasn't about to stop. Who knew that Al was a Confucius kind of guy?

March

Even before I started sewing a stitch, I had decided I would have the jumper ready to wear to my next writers' group meeting. After all, it was my only social life, so it was the only place I could wear it apart from the library where jeans worked best. I found that old sweats were the best everyday kind of attire for the job at hand – by which I mean basement clearing. I hadn't made it upstairs to the main floor or, god forbid, the attic, yet – but that was another job. In any case, I wasn't known for my sartorial savvy, which I suppose you've already figured out. Evelyn was the fashionable daughter; I assuredly was not. However, I was beginning to think that this sewing thing might change all that.

I followed directions from several different sources. First, there was the pattern itself that contained a surprisingly detailed guide, a fact that I ought to have remembered from my junior high days. *YouTube* was kind of like a sewing university for me. I was constantly amazed by the number of people who took the time to take pity on the rest of us who were so ignorant of the minutiae of whatever was their particular passion. In the case of people who sewed (who had started calling themselves "sewists" in recent years), there were thousands of videos to choose from. Keep in mind, though, that not all of them were useful. As I continued to discover, many were appallingly bad – poorly shot, poorly lit often with truly awful hosts who were disorganized or barely literate – or both. Anyway, after getting through a bunch of those, I stumbled on some truly exceptional ones. These were the ones where the host was knowledgeable, the video appeared to have been thought through in advance, and the execution was professional. These were the ones whose channels I subscribed to, and those are the ones that became my mentors. Of course, Grace turned out to be my favourite one.

After watching dozens of her videos, I found out that Grace was a woman from somewhere in the southern reaches of the United States. About as far from the reaches of the centre of the fashionista universe as you could get (Paris in my estimation), she had a kind of mesmerizingly soft yet capable voice. She was probably somewhere north of fifty years old, her reading specs perched beguilingly on the end of her nose and her tousled red hair of a hue that had never occurred in nature, Grace hypnotized me with her little snippets of sewing sagacity. Her mantra, one that she mentioned in every video and that was prominently displayed in what looked like a cross-stitch hanging on the wall behind her, was something the Dalai Lama seems to have said once upon a time. *Remember that not getting what you want is sometimes a wonderful stroke of luck.* I had not had that experience personally, but I was willing to keep an open mind.

As far as Grace was concerned, sewists (she had adopted that odd word) often went at their projects grasping for a particular result. She said not getting there was often the best thing that ever happened. I was beginning to think she was probably a Buddhist with a southern accent.

Anyway, the result of spending some quality time with Grace was that I was actually able to pull off a bit of a coup: I made the jumper, it fit me, and it didn't look terrible. To be honest about fit, when a piece of clothing is referred to as "flared," which is how this garment was described on the pattern envelope, what we're really talking about is a tent, isn't it? There's no getting around it. When it comes to tents, one-size-fits-nearly everyone. I would have to wear it when I next went to the fabric store. I somehow felt that I owed it to Al to let him see that his guidance had not been in vain.

So, when I arrived at Miriam's house the first Wednesday in March and removed my coat, I was expecting swoons of delight from my colleagues. After all, if artistic-type writers couldn't appreciate the creative aspect of making one's own clothing, then who could? As it turned out, it seemed I might have to look elsewhere for the positive reinforcement I seemed to be craving.

Joseph was first off the mark. "Charlie, darling, another tent?" he said as he poured the first round of wine into the mason jars Miriam liked to use for beverages of any kind.

Ignoring him, I stood up and took a model-like turn or at least my version of a turn I thought might be executed by a model on a run-way.

"That really doesn't help, you know. Are you planning to make all your future clothes?" Joseph snorted just a bit then daintily sipped his wine.

Miriam walked into the living room from her tiny galley kitchen. "Hmm...turn around again." She sipped her wine as she contemplated my tent. "Yes, slightly tent-like, but with a bit of drape this time. Corduroy, isn't it? And the colour. I do like that colour, Charlie. Well done."

Oh dear. Miriam seemed to be the only one who liked it. Again. This wasn't good, but in my defence, I actually felt good in it. It fit my shoulders and stood away from the rest of me – hiding everything I wanted to hide. I felt as if I could almost become invisible beneath it. I wondered what Wendy would have thought. She was among the missing this evening because of some calamity or other with her children. Then, I pondered about what Karl thought. He hadn't said a word.

Karl was sitting in a large wicker papa-san chair with its enormous blue cushion that could almost swallow you whole, sipping a beer from his mason jar.

He had a sheaf of papers on his lap and seemed to be actively trying to dodge the conversation by avoiding eye contact. He looked as if he were absorbed in his reading, but I could tell it was a ruse.

"So, Karl, what do you think? Everyone else has an opinion on my new approach to dressing."

"Oh, Charlie, I don't know anything about clothes. Whatever you like. It's your choice, isn't it?" He looked pointedly at Joseph, and then Miriam before turning his attention back to the papers in his lap.

"A bit holier-than-thou, aren't you?" Joseph clearly wasn't going to let Karl get away without comment so quickly. "I bet you do have an opinion."

"Karl?" I said. "I *would* really like to hear what you think."

He put his beer down on the tiny table next to the large chair and shifted his weight so that he was facing me. He leaned down to place the sheaf of papers on the floor, then sat up and looked at me. "You sure you really want to know what I think, Charlie?"

I nodded.

"Okay, but you're not going to like it."

Miriam sat down next to Joseph on the sofa, waiting for Karl to hold forth.

"I think you're trying really hard to be something you're not."

I was puzzled and possibly a bit defensive. "You'll have to do better than that, Karl. What am I not? Someone who sews her own clothes?"

"No, that's not what I mean. I mean that you're sewing things you think fit in with a writerly lifestyle if I can use that word. Take Miriam, for instance." He gestured toward Miriam, who was starting to purse her lips as if she might be preparing for an onslaught. "She's the real deal." Miriam half-smiled. "I mean, she's got this artistic thing down to a science." Miriam started to interrupt. "No disrespect intended, but let me finish," he said.

Karl sat up straighter – as straight as one can in one of those round chairs – and continued. "Have any of you read Henri Muger's *Scènes de la Vie de Bohème*?"

I sat down and picked up my mason jar, marvelling just slightly that he had read it. God, I was judgmental. "Wasn't that the story that the opera *La Bohème* is based on?"

"And the Broadway musical *Rent* as I recall," Joseph added.

"Have any of you read the original?"

We all mumbled something about our French not being up to it.

"Well, anyway, I have," Karl said, ignoring our open-mouthed stares as we considered his previously undiscovered language capabilities. "It's a story of four starving artists in Paris in the 1840s. It's where the stereotype of the starving artist developed. Sacrificing material aspects of life for your art and all that...and the bohemian kind of sartorial choices that have come to be associated with it."

Karl never ceased to amaze me. He may have driven a truck for a living, but there was no doubt about his artist's soul. And really, who has read *Scènes de la Vie de Bohème* anyway?

"Okay," I said, sipping my wine, "what does that have to do with my new jumper – or my new sewing projects?" I was a bit distracted by the fact that I'd never asked Karl anything about his education. I must have assumed that since he drove a truck for a living, he must have barely finished high school. This man did not sound like someone who had barely finished high school. Come to think of it, he never did. I was annoyed at myself for never having truly listened to him before. I jerked my mind back to the current conversation, making a note to ask him more about where he went to school.

"It has nothing to do with your sewing projects specifically," he said. "I think that it's a noble creative pursuit for you or anyone else. Creating your own clothes, I mean. What I'm referring to is that you seem to be trying too hard to appear to be what you believe an artist should be, or at least, should present to the world. You seem to be concerned about presenting an image."

I started to protest but was immediately unsure of what to say. Joseph helped me out. "Wait a minute, Karl," he said, sitting up to place his mason jar on the coffee table that was, by the way, a cross-section of some kind of a tree. "Are you trying to say that there's some preconceived stereotype of an artist?"

Karl looked at him thoughtfully. "Yup."

"Well, that's just a bit presumptuous, don't you think?" Miriam had now joined the conversation. "In point of fact, I am aware of the concept of archetypes. I *did* study Carl Jung in university back in the day, as they say, you know. And I don't remember any starving artist archetype among his theory of archetypes." She snorted. "In any case, it was only a theory." She looked pointedly at Karl. "You do know what a *theory* is, don't you?"

Oh dear, I thought, *please don't let this group come to blows. If it breaks apart, I'll lose my only lifeline to what passes for a social life.*

Karl seemed to let that little dig at his perceived lack of higher education slide off his back. It wasn't the first time the issue had come up. He had always ignored it, as I now recalled. I had long observed that he was very adept at the art of deflection. In any case, sometimes Miriam could be a bit of a cow if their past interactions were anything to go by.

"Technically, you're right, Miriam," Karl said, not taking the bait. He seemed to be warming to his topic. "Jung's original theory of human motivation contained only twelve fundamental archetypes. The starving artist was not one of them. But, as you also might remember from *back in the day*, they were divided into four major categories. Jung suggested that there are what he called 'Four Cardinal Orientations.' He believed that as individuals, we're motivated primarily by one of either ego, order, social concerns or freedom."

"I'm not familiar with this Carl Jung. How do you spell that?" Joseph said as he reached for his notebook and pen that he kept with him always. I spelled it for him. He continued. "This could be very useful to me. I'm trying to figure out a new character in my book. How to describe his motivation is eluding me. Carry on." He scribbled a few notes.

I was just happy that the conversation seemed to have moved away from my personal sartorial choices and on to a more esoteric conversation thread.

"Oh, yes, do continue, professor," Miriam said, sitting back against the sofa cushions crossing her arms against her ample bosom. I'm sure I detected more than a modicum of condescension in her tone.

Daggers were now shooting out of Karl's eyes at Miriam, but he would not be deterred. "For example, people who are explorer types or outlaw types are motivated largely by the need for freedom, but so are creators. The interesting thing about creators – and writers are, of course, creators – is that when Jung placed these Cardinal Orientations onto a kind of wheel, creators sit in the freedom section right up against the section where *ego* is the motivation. People who have elaborated on his theory have added several more nuanced archetypes, and the starving artist is among those newer ones. I think you can all see where I'm going with this."

"Not quite there yet," Joseph said. "Please continue. I feel a new character coming on."

Karl looked at Miriam as if for permission to continue. After all, she was hosting this evening. She nodded at him, her arms still firmly crossed.

"Starving artists are motivated by the desire for freedom to do what they want with a bit of ego thrown in. Actually, when you think about it, most artistic types do think they're a bit better than everyone else and just a bit entitled."

"That is so insulting," Miriam interjected.

"Maybe a bit," Karl said, "but if you're honest, you have to admit first that the starving artist type does exist, and second that there's an edge of moral superiority over other mere mortals."

"So, are you suggesting that I'm too self-righteous?" I said. At the risk of taking the conversation back to where it started – namely my tent – I did want to know.

I valued Karl's opinion, although I'm not sure why.

"No," he said, turning toward me. "As a matter of fact, it's just the opposite. I don't think you *are* that starving artist type, but I do think you would like to be."

He thought I wanted to starve? Did I want to be a starving artist? Who would want to starve? I was thinking. Maybe I had missed something.

"What about you?" Joseph looked up at Karl, his pen poised over his little green-covered notebook.

"Me? I'm no starving artist," Karl said. "Why do you think I drive a truck for a living?"

"Perhaps you don't think your writing is good enough to sustain you."

I looked at Miriam. We were back on thin ice here as a group, in my view. I wished that she might for once just shut up. Just once.

"Maybe, Miriam, but mostly I'm a pragmatist, and I like to be comfortable. And come to that, I want my family to be comfortable. I *am* the only one in the room with kids."

He was undoubtedly right about that since Wendy wasn't there. The other three of us couldn't be trusted with a puppy at this stage in our lives. Not even Miriam. Despite her scorn, she was probably the closest to the bohemian artist among us, and since she was older, she had a lot more experience being one than we did. But what *about* me? Was I trying to be something I wasn't? Was I so enthralled with the idea of the artist that I was willing to starve for my art? Was Evelyn right about me after all? I did have to face at least the facts, if not the truth: Mom had indeed been supporting my artistic habit. She was my moral support when I was young, and for the ten years since Dad died, financial. I had never really known why she was so supportive. I guess I didn't want to question it in case it stopped. And I always did think that success was right around the corner. I mean, how else does an artist carry on? You have to believe that the dream can come true. Don't you?

"Karl, I'm thinking about the dream of success that I think all of us in this room carry around with us. Isn't it this dream that keeps us going?" I said.

"Well, first of all, I think we all need to re-evaluate how we define success."

"Selling a book to a publisher?" Joseph said.

“Maybe that’s *your* dream,” Miriam said, “but my dream is bigger. Broader. I want nothing less that to influence the world.”

“That is broader,” Karl said. “And it does make the point that all our definitions of success are different. Maybe success for some writers is simply finishing something. The truth is that I’d like to believe that artistry that’s fuelled by dreams *and* pragmatism can coexist. I’d like to believe that I don’t have to sacrifice my creature comforts to be a successful writer,” Karl said. “Whatever that means to me – and you.”

I found myself agreeing with him.

~

When I arrived home later that evening, I walked into Mom’s bedroom where the only full-length mirror in the house lived. I stood there for a long time staring at myself, trying to figure out what someone might think if they didn’t know me. What I saw was a slightly dishevelled thirty-something woman with wild hair, large – some might say gaudy – earrings, a black turtleneck under a – tent. There was simply no other way to describe it. I was wearing a tent. A cheerless, inky blue, wide, all-concealing tent. It did hide a multitude and perhaps not just literally.

I lay down on Mom's bed for a minute and thought about the evening. We had said our good-byes gingerly. Interestingly, it was the first writers' group meeting where we hadn't taken the occasion to read any of our work at all. Instead, we discussed the issue of human motivation, which, as any writer knows, is at the root of character development in a novel, and we were all writing novels. I just had the feeling that we weren't talking about characters – at least not the ones on the pages of our works-in-progress.

~

I debated long and hard about whether or not I'd go back to see Al to show him this new creation. He had, after all, aided and abetted me on the project, but it had turned out to be another tent. Even I had to admit that. In the end, I popped it on under my long black winter coat, debated whether or not it was cold enough for ear muffs and headed back to *Sew Fine Things.*

When I opened the door, I could hear voices coming from the back. They were speaking in a language I didn't understand or even recognize. I realized that Al's almost imperceptible, slightly exotic, accented English probably spoke volumes about his provenance. As I felt my way along a line of fabric bolts, caressing each one under my fingertips as if I might be able to conjure up the perfect garment to be created from each one, I realized that I knew nothing about Al. But then, why should I? After all, he was simply a sales clerk in a fabric store. Yes, that was it. He had introduced me to a world I had never known existed.

I rounded a corner and ran headlong into an older woman in a colourful headscarf who seemed to be preoccupied with a large tote bag under her arm. She looked up quickly and muttered something like "sorry, so sorry" before hurrying off toward the door. The little wind chime on the door jangled happily as it closed behind her. I turned to see Al's head poking out the door to what must have been a back room. He looked a bit sheepish.

Running a hand through his dark hair, he seemed to realize that there was a customer in the store, so he smiled. "Good morning. How may I help you?' Then he did a bit of a double-take. "Charlie, isn't it? So sorry. I didn't realize that it was you. Please come in. I have some remnants to show you."

It was clear he wasn't prepared to explain the woman who he had plainly been arguing with, and then again, why should he? It was none of my business. I followed him to the front of the store where he had a box full of bolt ends of fabrics: those left-over pieces that can no longer be measured out from a bolt.

"I've been thinking about you," he said as he took four or five bundles out of the box, placing them side by side on the counter. "I saw this piece of velvet and thought you might like to learn to sew something a bit more exotic than a corduroy jumper. By the way, how did that project work out?"

I unbuttoned my coat and slid it off my shoulders, placing it on the counter. I tried to gauge his reaction, but his face remained passive. I did a little twirl, and when I turned back toward him, I could see the almost imperceptible curve of a smile. But it was his eyes, once again, that gave him away. There was little doubt that he was laughing.

"Well," I said. "What do you think? Be honest."

"Charlie," Al said now smiling broadly, "it's…it's…what's the word?"

"A tent?"

"Well, I was going to say that it seems a bit too big for you."

"A tent by any other name," I said, picking up my coat. I suddenly had a tremendous compulsion to hide the tent, or perhaps hide myself. I knew it wasn't my best look. Why did I keep making and wearing these tent-like creations?

"You've done a commendable job on this garment," he said, reverting to his fabric-guru-sales-clerk persona. "Are you interested in learning more? Moving on to a new challenge?"

I was and said so. As I ran my hand over various textures represented in the little pile of remnants on the counter, I realized that I had a considerable urge to see what could be fashioned out of one or more of these pieces. There seemed to be so much possibility here. All at once, they represented a vast unknown journey that I might miss out on if I ignored them.

"Did you bring along any more of your mother's vintage patterns?"

I rummaged in my backpack, withdrawing four patterns which I then placed on the counter. At this point, I had already counted Mom's collection, and if I had found all of them, she had been saving a whopping 150 patterns! And I had no real idea whether or not there might be more secreted away somewhere among the boxes in the basement and – *dear god I had forgotten! What about the attic?* I couldn't think about that right now, but I'd get back to it.

"Fantastic," Al said, beaming as he picked up each one, in turn, examining the front illustrations then turning each one over. On the back were the line drawings of the designs and the small print telling you how much fabric would be required for each view.

"You said your mother had dozens."

"Actually," I said, taking my backpack off the counter and placing it on a stool next to it, "I've found about 150."

Al whistled softly. "What a treasure. So, Charlie," he said, "how did you pick these ones?"

I told him I had chosen two of them randomly by sticking my hand in a box and picking two as if I might be selecting a prizewinner from a jar of ticket stubs. The other two took a bit more thought. I looked at several dozen and chose the ones that seemed to draw me in.

"Which one are you planning for your next project?" Al said as he lined them all up on the counter facing me. He sat back on the stool behind the counter and waited.

"Well, of course, the two I chose deliberately are the two I'm most drawn to. But..."

"But, they're both almost identical to the shapeless piece you made last month?"

Geez, how does this man I hardly know seem to know me so well? I thought.

"Or because they look easy?"

"Easy is good," I said. "Let's go with easy." I really didn't like the thought of being drawn to shapelessness.

"Someone once told me that there are always two choices. One of those choices is the easy way. But the only reward you get from taking the easy way is that it's easy."

I thought about that for a moment. "Okay, if I don't choose an easy one, how do I choose?"

Al moved one of the patterns toward me. "Is this one of the ones that spoke to you?"

I shook my head. It had not. In fact, when I picked it out of the box randomly, I almost put it back. I hadn't looked at it carefully. Now I noted that it was another one of those ones called "Jiffy" patterns. The fact that it was called "Jiffy" should have beckoned me toward it. After all, jiffy suggested fast, straightforward, uncomplicated, undemanding. In a word, easy. There it was again – easy. But the style just didn't seem to be "me."

"Al, I might be able to learn to make this one, but I wouldn't be able to wear it. So, what's the point?"

He looked puzzled. "Why couldn't you wear it? At least when the weather warms up?"

It looked like a dress that someone with a much more sophisticated life might wear. It had what seemed to me like bell-shaped sleeves that stopped just below the elbow and a neckline with a little slit in the front. It was a simple dress, and yet it had a kind of elegance that didn't match the picture I had of myself in my head. I'm an artist, after all, not a lady who lunches. *Geez*, I thought, *maybe Karl was right about me.* I just didn't know how to express this to Al.

"It's really not *me*, I guess. I mean, I'm a writer."

Al looked puzzled, and I realized that he didn't know much about me at all.

"Yeah, an artist. And, you know what artists are like," I said.

"Of course, you're an artist," he said. "I knew that the moment you walked in the door."

"My wardrobe choices gave me away, didn't they?"

He shook his head. "Not at all. It wasn't your wardrobe at all. If I had judged you by your wardrobe when I first met you, I would not have concluded that you're an artist."

It was my turn to be puzzled. I was also a bit concerned about what conclusion he might have drawn based on my wardrobe, but I chose not to ask. I think I didn't want to know.

"Charlie, what's more important to you: being who you're supposed to be – in other words, being yourself – or having others think something in particular?"

I had never thought of that. I always thought of Evelyn as the one whose decisions were profoundly affected by what she thought other people might think. I had always taken a dim view of that perspective. I liked to think of myself as a free spirit who didn't care what others thought, whose life wasn't influenced by external forces. Was I kidding myself?

Since I didn't answer, Al continued. "You know the work of Niccolò Machiavelli?"

I knew that one of my philosophy professors had forced us to read a book he wrote. It was called *The Prince,* throughout which the author espoused an approach to life that didn't sit well with me. After all, who could like someone whose essential personal philosophy suggested that it was okay to disregard morality and deceive even your closest friends and allies all in the interest of achieving your goals?

"I know what you're thinking. You think that there is nothing to be learned from someone like Machiavelli."

That about covers it, I thought.

"We may not agree with his overall philosophy," Al said, "but he did have some brilliant insights."

Who is this fabric store clerk, anyway? I thought as Al talked. This question only added to my increasing feeling that I didn't seem to know any of the people in my life. Karl? Yeah, him. Maybe even Mom.

He pointed to a small empty space on the wall behind the counter where there were no bolts of fabric. Nestled between the shelves was a small wooden frame. Inside the frame was what looked from a distance to be an embroidered wall-hanging. It read: *Everyone sees what you appear to be, few experience what you really are.*

"Machiavelli?"

He nodded. "And, '*Trust not too much to appearances.*'" He looked at my face, which, no doubt, conveyed complete bewilderment. "Virgil."

Where did he come up with all this wisdom? Because I suddenly realized, as if I had been struck with lightning, that he was right.

"So, Al, do you have any fabric you'd recommend for this project?"

He smiled broadly. "Well, then, step right this way, mademoiselle."

~

Karl had become such a good friend to me. Several days after I had happily returned home with a beautiful piece of deep burgundy-coloured piqué with which I would make that "Jiffy" dress (even if it killed me), I realized that I had made quite a bit of progress with clearing out Mom's basement. There were only a few boxes of items I had deemed worthy of keeping and oddly several pieces of furniture that had been completely hidden from view left. They had to be carted upstairs, so I decided to take Karl up on his offer to help with the heavy lifting – in this case, literally. He didn't hesitate one moment to come to my aid. So, on Saturday afternoon, with the promise of beer and pizza at the end, Karl came over to help with lifting said objects upstairs and moving a few more large pieces from the main floor into a rental van so I could donate them to a local charity on Monday morning.

"Is your wife okay with you spending the afternoon with me?" I asked as we moved the first piece of furniture, a glass étagère (yes, I know, how could it have been hidden in the basement?) carefully up the stairs.

"She's taken the kids to a birthday party. And I've told her about you, anyway."

"Yikes, Karl. What precisely have you told your wife about me?"

"Oh, just that you're a writer with the soul of a fashion designer."

I almost swallowed my tongue at this characterization. I coughed slightly. "Fashion designer?" I looked around the shelving to see if I could catch his eye. He was smiling broadly.

"Well, you have to admit that your recent sartorial choices suggest a bent in that direction."

"Yeah," I said, hoisting my load up another step, "about that. And what was all that about the starving artist?"

"I stand by what I said." We had reached the top of the stairs. "Where do you want this?"

I pointed to the dining room. When we got it into the room and up against a wall, I sat down on a dining room chair and caught my breath.

"Karl," I said as he wiped the glass of the cabinet with a cloth I had taken out for this purpose, "if you don't mind my asking, where did you pick up all that stuff about Carl Jung?"

He sat down opposite me and placed his clasped hands on the table. "I don't mind you asking, actually." He sat back. "I studied it in grad school."

I tried not to look as surprised as I felt. Grad school? How many truck drivers have been to grad school?

"Grad school?" I began carefully. "Where did you go to grad school?"

"The University of Arizona."

"You're an American?" Where in the world did that come from? I seemed to have put my mouth in gear before my brain. What difference did that make to the topic at hand?

He just laughed. “Actually, no. I’m a red-blooded Canadian, through and through. You’ve seen my plaid shirts. That proves it, doesn’t it?”

I laughed. “Touché.” Then I got serious. “You’ve never mentioned any of this before.”

“No one has ever asked,” he said, shrugging.

He was right. I had known Karl for about seven years worth of writers’ group evenings, but we had never had a single discussion about his background. I guess we just thought that since he was a truck driver. Not that there was anything wrong with that. If anything, I had always been impressed by him given his “situation” as a truck driver-husband-father-breadwinner. Or at least that’s what I thought. I didn’t know quite what to think at this juncture.

“You know, Charlie, people aren’t always what they appear to be. Not me. Not even you.”

“Trust not too much to appearances,” I said softly, quoting Al quoting Virgil.

“What was that?

“Oh, just something someone said to me a few days ago. Trust not too much to appearances.”

“Virgil?”

I nodded, impressed again. Then I looked at the clock on the wall above the dining room door. "I think it's time for a beer and time for you to tell me all about grad school."

"Well," he said, "it all started back where I grew up in Northern Ontario in a family who had never had anyone go to university."

Two hours later, we had polished off a couple of beers and a large pepperoni pizza, and I was awestruck – stunned by the revelation that I had never known anything at all about this man I had called a friend for so long.

I now knew a lot more about Karl than merely where he'd grown up.

April

APRIL

April Fools' Day. Every April first, when I wake up in the morning, even after all these years, I still expect Mom's head to pop in through my bedroom door, a slightly alarmed look on her face.

"My word, Charlie, it snowed so much last night. Better get your snowsuit out for school!" And then she would abruptly disappear to greet Evelyn with the same dire weather report.

I would jump out of bed and race to the window – it had been such a lovely spring day yesterday, and I was so looking forward to wearing my new shoes. I would fling the curtains open and groan as I felt more than saw Mom in the doorway again. I could almost feel that grin beginning to creep from her lips to her eyes.

"April fool!" she would shout with glee then quickly head off down the hall to the kitchen. She caught me every time.

This year when I awoke on April 1, I didn't immediately get up to see what awaited me outside my window, although I thought about it. I was still ruminating about Karl's' story. It was the first thought I'd had every morning since he had told me a week ago. I was more stunned by the realization that I *did* draw so many conclusions from appearances. What's more, I had begun to think he might be right about me, too. I was no longer so sure I was what I appeared to be. At least I was beginning to see.

Considering that I had long regarded Karl as a friend, I was almost embarrassed to discover how little of consequence I really knew about him. I was still boggled by the knowledge that I had been so utterly unaware of his life as a Ph.D. student. I was perhaps even more astonished that he had gotten caught up in a nasty fight with his research supervisor who refused to sign his dissertation defence, effectively ending his academic career. I could not imagine what it must have been like to have completed all those years of study, and all that research, only to have your fate controlled by a single person whose power held sway over a committee – a group whose approval meant the difference between successfully acquiring the doctorate or not. It was an all or nothing prospect. Either you were granted your Ph.D. on the successful defence of your dissertation, or it was up and out, as they say. Either your dissertation was given a passing grade, or you were out of the program. There were no second chances. Karl was out. And it seemed he had never looked back.

Karl met Julie, the love of his life, when he was in grad school. She was a student in nutrition science, and they fell head over heels in love. She had supported his decision to leave academia while she carried on and completed her own doctorate. I had no idea that Julie was a professor while Karl drove a truck. He told me that he had no regrets, though. What he had really wanted to do all along was be a novelist – and a dad.

I was still thinking about Karl when I went to the window to open the curtains. I could hardly believe my eyes! Was I hallucinating? There in front of me was a thick mantle of clean, white snow. I could feel my mother breathing down my neck, laughing softly. Then, as if she were right there whispering in my ear, I heard a voice say, “Finish it,” so softly that I almost missed it. I jerked my head around, and of course, there was no one there.

Finish it? I thought. *Is that you, Mom, trying to tell me something from beyond the grave? And finish what?* Chills ran down my spine.

~

Finish it. This was the one thought swirling around in my mind as I poured boiling water over the instant coffee crystals I was opting for this morning instead of Nespresso™. Then, as I stirred milk into the muddy coffee in the big, blue mug I'd found at the back of one of Mom's kitchen cupboards, my mind began to flit from one thing to another. Finish what? There were so many things. Where to begin?

I sat down with my faux-coffee and chewed on a piece of buttered toast. (Have I told you how much I love toast? A strange passion, perhaps, but it's mine.) I reached for a pen and the steno pad that Mom had always kept in the kitchen drawer for making grocery lists and started to make my own list.

Finish cleaning up the house. That was a given, but it didn't seem to fulfil the directive.

Finish...finish...what?

I was going to have to start thinking outside the box as the saying goes.

Finish the magazine article I'd been working on for the past six months? Who takes six months to write a magazine piece? I'd never make a living as a freelance magazine writer at that rate.

Finish the piece I'd proposed to an online magazine a few days before Mom died? The editor said she was interested, but I had never gotten back to her. At this point, I knew she probably wasn't interested anymore – at least not in a writer who couldn't follow up within a reasonable period of time.

Finish the three unfinished novels that were sitting on my computer hard drive? Who am I kidding? If any of them had been any good or had even interested me for long enough, I would have finished at least one of them long ago. My ideas were so lame, it seemed. Even my writing group yawned when I read from them.

All of which brought me right back to where I had started: finish cleaning up the house? Well, that was a given: it had to be done sooner or later.

Somehow, I didn't believe it was any of these. I'd have to think about that later. This morning I had made a specific appointment with Al to show him the dress I'd finished last week. It was still too cold to wear it, but I was so excited about having made something that looked like a real dress.

~

When I arrived at the shop, I was greeted by the woman who had been hurrying out when I'd been here the last time. Today she was sporting a beautiful green and blue silk headscarf that perfectly matched her blue silk dress. The dress resembled a floor-length shirt with long sleeves. She was wearing it with a wide leather belt. I thought I recognized the blue silk from a bolt I'd seen on Al's counter last month. I wondered how old she was. She looked to me to be anywhere from thirty to fifty.

"May I help you?" she said. Her accent sounded a bit exotic – as if perhaps middle-eastern-via-England – sort of like Al's accent but not quite. "Oh," she said as if she suddenly recognized me, "you must be looking for Alvaro." I must have looked puzzled.

"I suppose he told you his name was Al?" She shook her head slightly, and I think she may even have tut-tutted a bit. "I will get him." And she disappeared into the far reaches of the back of the store.

I wandered down my favourite aisle while I was waiting. It was lined with colourful bolts of what Al had told me was silk charmeuse. After the first time I'd run my hand over the incredible silky softness of this shimmering fabric, I had gone home to do some online research about it. Al had told me that it could be quite challenging to work with (a bit like some people I knew. Evelyn came immediately to mind). This only made me more determined to set my sights on making something with it in the future. If I didn't miss my guess, I'd wager that the woman's headscarf and dress were both made of silk charmeuse. I watched her glide away in a shimmer of light reflecting a single beam of sunshine that had made its way in through a small, clean space of window glass.

"Charlie!"

I turned to see Al coming toward me carrying three large bolts of fabric. He was smiling so widely I could see his perfect white teeth. I looked behind him to see if the mysterious woman might have returned. He glanced over his shoulder, perhaps to see what had caught my gaze.

"Good morning, Charlie." He put his burden on the counter but didn't mention the mysterious woman at all. "Nice to see you. I've got some great new fabric, and I'll show you mine if you show me yours." Did he wink?

I think I might have blushed. "You mean Mom's vintage patterns?"

"That and your project. Are you wearing it?"

I looked down at my black parka that I hadn't yet let go of on this bright April morning. "Well, I did finish the dress, but it's really more of a summer thing."

"I suppose. But did you bring it?"

I had brought it. I put my backpack on the counter beside the bolts of fabric and opened it slowly as if preparing for the "reveal."

Al sat down on a small wooden stool behind the counter while I pulled the dress out of my backpack and ceremoniously unfolded it. Since the dress was constructed of only two large pieces cut out in the shape of the main dress with the flared sleeves attached, it had been easy to accomplish. The fact that it had a little slit in the front of the neckline also meant that it could fit over my head without the help of a zipper. This was a good thing for someone who couldn't remember how to put a zipper in a dress and had found the online video instructions confusing in the extreme.

When I laid it out flat on the counter, he leaned forward and picked up a sleeve, looking closely at the hem.

"I know it's not perfect," I said. "I mean, I'll never be as good as most of the people who shop in here..." I trailed off. I wasn't sure what I was trying to say. I had never thought about getting "good" at sewing. In fact, it seemed as if I'd never concerned myself about getting "good" at anything other than writing, now that I thought about it. Was I really that much of a one-note person?

Al put the sleeve down and looked at me. He smiled slightly. "Charlie, you don't need to compare yourself to anyone else."

Was I doing that?

"What about another pattern? What are you planning to make next?"

I pulled out three more patterns. "I kind of like these," I said, but I was still distracted by his comment suggesting that I compared myself to others.

Al leaned over the counter to examine the patterns. He looked at the front of each envelope briefly but spent a lot more time looking at the drawings on the back. "This one," he said finally, tapping on the illustration on the front of the pattern envelope. "This is the one you should do next."

I picked it up to examine it more closely. The colourful drawing on the front depicted three smiling young women, all wearing versions of an A-line mini-dress. It was clearly a pattern from the early 1970s.

One version of the dress had long sleeves with no collar, one had long sleeves with a collar, and one was sleeveless. I placed it back down on the counter between the two of us.

Al pointed to the version with long sleeves and no collar. “I have just the fabric in mind for this one.”

I was skeptical. What would I do with another dress? And more to the point, this one had a zipper in the back. Horror! I’d have to try to retrieve any memories I had of how to get that sucker in and return to those befuddling videos. I hadn’t come upon hers yet, but I was hoping that Grace might have one.

Al looked at me as if he could read my mind. “You can do this, Charlie.”

“I suppose,” I said, gazing at the pattern. “But it’ll be crap. I’m not sure I can pull this off.” My mind wandered away.

“Are we still talking about sewing this dress?” Al said, placing his palms down on the counter and leaning in slightly.

“What do you mean?”

“Well, Charlie, you’ve told me about your daunting task of having to clear out your mother’s house. And you’ve also told me about your writing. And your writing group and how you don’t think your writing measures up.”

“Well, it doesn’t,” I said somewhat too defensively even in my own estimation. “Even Miriam writes better than I do.”

Al stood up straight. “Do you always measure your success against the success of others?”

What in the world was he getting at? We were only talking about sewing, after all. Or were we?

Al turned around toward a small wall-mounted shelf behind the counter and retrieved a slim volume I hadn’t noticed before. He placed it on the counter so that I could read the title. *Tao Te Ching*. “You’ve read this book?” he said.

I shook my head. “Something old and Chinese?” It rang a distant bell somewhere in the far reaches of my memory. It seemed to evoke a memory of sitting in the back of a massive theatre classroom, nodding off while a professor way up front droned on about something.

He tapped on the title. “Yes, it is Chinese. From the sixth century. It roughly translates from the Chinese as ‘the way of integrity’ or ‘the way of virtue.’”

"Uh-huh." I could feel my eyes beginning to glaze over. I liked Al, so I tried as hard as I could to pay attention. Not one of my best-honed skills, it has to be said. Paying attention, that is.

Al tipped his head slightly and looked me straight in the face. "It really could be useful, you know, Charlie."

I snapped back to attention. "Please," I said as graciously as I could, hoping he hadn't noticed my nodding off. (I'm quite sure he did.) "I do want to hear about it."

"Well, the central theme of the book is that we all need to be more aware not of the world, as we've been told by certain modern gurus. We need to be more aware of ourselves."

"Isn't that kind of narcissistic?"

"Not really." He opened the book and pointed to a passage. "'*When you are content to be simply yourself and don't compare or compete, everyone will respect you.*'"

I thought about this for a split second before the penny dropped as the expression goes.

"I guess I have been comparing my work to others." Al seemed to almost look through me as I spoke. "Maybe I've even been comparing myself to others in general. I always seem to come up short." I thought about Evelyn. I always came up short beside her.

Al sat back down on the little stool and smiled. He crossed his arms. "'*Respect yourself and others will respect you.*' Confucius. See? Everyone says so."

I left the store forty-five minutes later with a new bundle of happy yellow linen safely tucked into my backpack. Oh, and yes, also a yellow zipper. I shuddered as I exited the door with a tinkle of bells. As I turned to walk toward the bus stop, I saw that there was a large placard in the corner of *Sew Fine's* window. It said, "*Can anything be sadder than work left unfinished? Yes, work never begun.* Christina Rossetti." And the whispered words filled my head again: *Finish it.*

~

I was still thinking about Al's odd words and that funny little voice in my head as I cleaned up the kitchen and got to work on the final boxes in the basement. As I looked around, I had to admit that I was really making some progress now and given that Evelyn had emailed to say she'd be arriving today, it wasn't a moment too soon.

My monkey mind then jumped to Evelyn and the many times she had mocked my attempts to make a living as a writer. I was so deep in thought that I knocked a box down from the last layer against the far wall. I didn't duck fast enough as a result of which it hit my cheek as it tumbled to the ground. It wasn't exactly like all the other boxes, though. It was a lot flatter. This one was heavy cardboard about three-feet square and six inches deep. I bent down to examine it. As if it might be a Christmas present, I picked it up and shook it. No clue there.

It was tightly sealed with what looked to be duct tape that I'd definitely need my box cutter to open. I was about to turn it over when I heard a noise upstairs. Damn, she was here! I laid it on the floor, rubbed my face hoping that it didn't look as if someone had slugged me and got up to greet my dear sister.

When I emerged from the basement into the kitchen, Evelyn was bending down into the refrigerator. A large suitcase (how long was she planning on staying?) and an expensive-looking carry-on whose provenance I didn't – but probably should – recognize were on the floor.

"I'm famished," she said. "Anything good to eat?"

"Hello to you, too," I said, opening an upper cupboard to retrieve two wine glasses. We were going to need wine and lots of it. I could feel it in my bones.

Then I opened a bag of chips that had been languishing on the countertop waiting for just the right moment for me to dive into my favourite comfort food. Now was the time. And I knew Evelyn was always so careful about her weight that she wouldn't touch a single one – that would be after she admonished me for chowing down on empty calories. Imagine my surprise when she stood up, looked at me and said, "I'll get the wine. Pour some of those chips in a bowl for me, too."

I was speechless. This was going to be interesting. As I got a bowl down from the upper cupboard for her (I was planning on eating from the bag), I realized that there was something different about Evelyn. She looked – how can I put this politely – dishevelled. Rumpled even. Her usually perfectly bobbed hair looked slightly greasy and messy, and she wasn't wearing her usual airplane attire – an all-black, tailored pantsuit. Today she was wearing jeans tucked into flat boots and a cardigan over something. I don't think I had seen Evelyn wearing a cardigan since we were pre-teens. What had come over her?

"What are you wearing?" Wasn't that what she had said to me (minus the F-word) the last time she arrived?

"Wearing?" Evelyn looked puzzled. "I'm wearing jeans and a sweater. What are you wearing? Not another shower curtain, I hope?"

In fact, I was wearing jeans and a cardigan. It looked as if we had conferred on our wardrobe choices before dressing in identical outfits.

"Where's your suit? And pumps?"

"Charlie, I just spent two hours crammed into an airplane with copious numbers of smelly people and wailing babies. The man next to me had halitosis that was not to be believed, and the kid behind me wouldn't stop kicking my seat back no matter how many times I gave him the stink eye. I spilled my wine down the front of my shirt," she said, pointing to the nasty red-wine stain on the cream-coloured silk shirt the cardigan had been covering up. "And I broke a fingernail getting my carry-on bag out of the overhead bin." She looked on the verge of tears.

I could not stand the thought of watching Evelyn break down again, so I quickly poured her a large glass of whatever chardonnay was in the bottle she'd found in the fridge. I thrust it at her since she seemed to have forgotten that she had taken on wine-pouring duties. What was especially puzzling to me was that none of her tale of woe – not a single aspect of it – made the slightest bit of sense to me. It certainly did not explain why she had gotten onto the plane wearing an outfit she would typically not be caught dead in, nor why she clearly seemed to have been flying economy rather than business class, as was her usual choice. The truth was that I didn't know how to broach the subject to her, either.

She took the glass from me and gulped half of it down at one go while still standing beside the table. She then slumped into a chair and guzzled the rest of it. "Another," she said, holding her glass out to me.

I complied, then I took the seat across from her and daintily sipped from my own glass. I cleared my throat as I watched her close her eyes and take another long swallow. "Evelyn," I began carefully, "are you okay?"

"What do you mean?" Her eyes flew open, and she very nearly spat at me.

"I just mean...well...you don't usually gulp your wine." *There*, I thought, *that should be innocuous enough.*

"What the f**k do you know?" She put the glass down on the table near the edge.

I wanted to shuffle across and push it back so that it didn't topple onto the floor but decided to stay put given her frame of mind. She might punch me. I waited. I didn't know how to continue anyway.

"What the actual f**k does anyone really know about anyone?"

Was this a rhetorical question? Probably, but I couldn't let that go. "'*Everyone sees what you appear to be, few experience what you really are,'"* I said more to myself than to her. It was for my benefit anyway.

"What the hell are you mumbling about," Evelyn said, reaching for the wine bottle. She poured out the last of it and started to sip a bit more slowly now.

"Just something a friend said to me."

"I've heard it somewhere before."

"I have no doubt," I said. "It's a Machiavelli quote."

She suddenly seemed deflated. "Few experience who you really are," she repeated. She laughed in one of those creepy kinds of laughs you hear on horror movies just before something truly terrifying happens.

"Evelyn," I said, summoning up all the chutzpa I could manage, "what's going on? You don't look like yourself, you're not acting like yourself, and if I had to guess, I'd say you're drunk."

"Well," she said, twirling a strand of greasy hair, "that's the answer. I'm drunk." With that, she drained her glass and started looking around for more.

I knew that I wasn't going to get anywhere with her tonight. I pretended that there wasn't any more wine – or anything else she might find an acceptable substitute – and trundled her off to bed. She fell onto her old mattress that was still covered with a duvet she'd picked out in high school, and didn't move. I took off her shoes and stashed her carry-on bag in the corner, turned off the lamp and closed the door. Tomorrow – round two.

The next day dawned bright and sunny, and Evelyn seemed to have miraculously recovered.

I was just pouring myself a cup of coffee when she flounced into the kitchen fresh from the shower with her hair sleek and shiny once again, wearing a pair of dark-wash skinny jeans, a soft pink cashmere pullover and a jaunty silk scarf. "Coffee smells good," she said. "Any bagels?"

And just like that, yesterday was a dream – or more like a nightmare if you want the honest truth.

We ate breakfast together without a single mention of her behaviour the day before. I just didn't know how to open the conversation and wasn't at all sure I wanted to go there anyway. She read a few text messages as she ate but, for the most part, stayed in the moment with me. We chatted about any number of inconsequential things.

"Well," she said finally, "I guess we better get to it." She rinsed her dishes then put them in the dishwasher. "Okay, Charlie, it's time to get this house sold."

Geez, I thought, *she has no earthly idea of how much more work needs to be done.* I supposed she really meant it was time to divide up Mom's Bakelite.

We had both always adored it. Mom had only ever worn it on special occasions, although I have no idea why. To me, it seemed more like everyday jewelry. Even so, we remembered it well. Ever since either of us could remember, Mom had kept her stash of Bakelite in the bottom drawer of her dresser. I hadn't yet gotten to her bedroom – I had been avoiding it, preferring to stick to the basement – but it was time for Evelyn and I to begin to figure out what we'd do with her personal things. Despite Evelyn's matter-of-fact, business-like approach that she seemed to be relying on this morning, I was glad that I wasn't doing this by myself.

We had decided on her last visit to take all the pieces, lay them out on Mom's bed and figure out how to divide them up. I knew that Evelyn had a few favourite pieces – she had made that abundantly clear all throughout our teen years and even this morning.

"You remember Mom's bangle watch with the Bakelite strap?"

I did, indeed, remember it. The round watch face was set into the translucent amber material, and I loved it. It had been one of the pieces I had fancied the most.

"I want that," she said as if calling dibs like a child picking a chocolate from a box.

I had been expecting this, but I wanted it, too. This wasn't going to be easy. But, then again, nothing with Evelyn was ever easy.

So, now we stood at the bottom of the bed where the pieces covered the tie-dyed duvet cover that Mom had been using for the past five or six years. The watch was there in its own box beside a plastic box of bangles. There were those ubiquitous amber Bakelite bangles, but there were also orange ones, yellow ones, and green ones. Mom used to stack them up on our arms when we begged her. I could still hear the sound they made when the clacked together. It was a sound that would always remind me of Mom. She let us try them on once in a while but rarely wore them herself. I could feel my eyes beginning to fill with tears. I sniffed.

There were also other non-jewelry pieces in Mom's collection. "Here," Evelyn said, picking up a black and turquoise radio. "You should have this."

How magnanimous of you, I thought. But, of course, I knew why she was doing it. It was so that she could claim the watch. I sighed. I did love that little radio, and it *would* look fantastic on a shelf in my someday home.

It took us the entire morning to make our decisions. Each time we'd pick up a piece, or a plastic box containing several small pieces, we'd begin to reminisce about what each one evoked in our memories of those times Mom had opened the collection to show it to us.

When we were finished, we had two large cardboard boxes with a reasonably even division of the pieces. I was wearing one of Mom's necklaces – with large, gold baubles – as we carried the boxes into the living room. Evelyn had opened her large suitcase and left it in the middle of the floor. It turns out it was almost empty. She had been planning on using it to transport her haul home to her condo. I wondered what the perfect, and perfectly fastidious Michael would think. Remember Michael?

Michael Jason Campbell-Watson III. Evelyn's husband. Well, the less said about him the better. She, of course, liked him but I never had. Michael came from money, but his father was a tightwad, so his son never did really see any of it beyond his private school education and the occasional trip abroad. He and Evelyn prided themselves in being "self-made." Michael was a stockbroker, whatever that was – I had very little idea of what went on in the higher echelons of high finance. I had, however, always suspected that Evelyn herself, who was building a successful career as a criminal lawyer in a fancy downtown law firm, made more money than he did. I often wondered what effect that might have had on the dynamics of their relationship. Of course, my interest was purely literary – they would make terrific characters in a novel.

I put my own box down on the living room floor and patted the beads on the necklace around my neck. "Do you think Bakelite is toxic?" I said.

"Where did that come from? Have your writer friends been waxing poetic about the environment again?"

"What? No. I just did a bit of research on the stuff, and it seems it's made from things like formaldehyde and asbestos from what I read."

"So what?"

"Well," and I was just thinking out loud here, "maybe it caused Mom's illness."

Evelyn stopped her activity of wrapping and packing Bakelite pieces and looked disdainfully at me. "What the actual f**k are you talking about, Charlie Hudson? Of course, it didn't. Get a life." She turned back to the packing. End of conversation.

The two of us spent the afternoon going through items in the dining room. We had three boxes labelled keep, toss and donate. The donate box was winning. After a dinner of take-out pizza (again) and another bottle of wine, we both called it an early night. By the time I got up the next morning Evelyn was already packed and ready to roll.

She checked her watch as I came into the kitchen. “My cab will be here in six minutes. Anything else you need me to do?”

It was all I could do to keep from shouting, “And what precisely do you expect to accomplish in six minutes?” But I didn’t.

“Charlie, when do you think you’ll actually have the house ready to stage?”

“Honestly, Evelyn, I don’t know. I haven’t even gotten to the attic yet.”

Evelyn looked out the window. “Got to go. I’ll expect an update next week. It’s almost May for god’s sake.”

And without another admonishment to me to get with the program and get the job finished, she was gone. I sank gratefully into a kitchen chair and contemplated my next move. *To the sewing machine*, I thought. *Junior* (remember I named my sewing machine?) *awaits!*

May

Who doesn't love the month of May? If you live in the northern hemisphere, that is. The birds are singing, the buds are bursting, and the air just feels so much more inviting. It makes you want to get outside. It certainly doesn't encourage holing up in an attic, but I knew that it had to be done.

I couldn't remember ever being up in the attic before. Not even Christmas decorations had been stored there. Mom and Dad had hauled them up from the basement every single year of my childhood. It was almost the only time Dad ever even ventured into the basement. I was actually wondering if the attic might not be empty. Maybe it wasn't even really an attic. At least that's what I hoped. Then I wouldn't have to empty it like I had been doing in the basement.

I sincerely hoped I'd find nothing. I hoped in vain.

I somehow managed to maneuver Dad's old aluminum ladder up from the basement where it had been collecting dust for years. It was only ever used by workers who came to fix things in the house. Dad was never a Mr. Fix-it kind of guy. I hauled it down the hall to just outside Mom's bedroom door and laid it on the floor. I was eternally grateful that this was a bungalow, which meant I didn't have to get it up another flight of stairs. The fact that this was a bungalow, however, means that the attic was likely enormous, covering the entire footprint of the house itself, much like the cavernous basement.

I managed to get the ladder in position leaning against the lip of the opening and climbed up. The "door" was really just a piece of plywood that I had to push up and over to access whatever lay above. I poked my head up through the hole very gingerly. I had visions of rats or mice crawling around up there even though I realized that if there were any critters up there, I would surely have heard their activity over the winter months. Well, there were no critters immediately visible, so I took my flashlight and tried to find a light switch. I sincerely hoped there was one. I finally located it on the wall stud just to my left.

I flicked it on. Like magic, a single, naked bulb hanging on a wire illuminated the musty, old space. And what was there in front of me? Boxes, boxes and more boxes. And dust. Dust motes seemed to billow from the surfaces like a kind of ground fog. I wondered how long had it been since anyone had been up here. Years, by the look of things.

I coughed and sputtered as I raised myself up until I was sitting on the edge. As I looked around, I began wondering how the hell I was supposed to get the boxes down. How in the world had Mom and Dad accumulated such a lot of stuff? I got myself up and moved carefully across the floor.

I crouched down beside the first box. I dislodged a thick layer of dust as I proceeded to pull pieces of yellowed tape off one of them to try to get a sense of what might be up here.

The box seemed to be full of...sewing patterns? More sewing patterns? What the heck? Who *was* this person I had called Mom for all my life? I shone my flashlight into the open box to get a better look.

Lifting the top envelope from the box, I noted that there was something different about these ones. They weren't tidy and flat like the ones I had found in the basement boxes. These were kind of tattered and fat as if someone had stuffed the tissue paper patterns back in after refolding them. At this point, I had learned enough about sewing patterns to recognize ones that had been cut. Someone had used these ones. It couldn't possibly have been my mother. Could it?

I looked around at the masses of boxes surrounding the opening where I was still sitting on the ledge. How was I going to get all of these down? And I knew I would have to. No one would buy a house where the attic was full of old, dusty and mouldering cardboard boxes.

I slid the box I'd already opened closer to me. I looked at it then at the access hole. It looked as if it would fit. *Well, of course, it will fit through, Charlie*, I thought, *someone got it up here*. Then, maybe, I could start down the ladder, maneuver it over my head and slide it down the ladder. It seemed like my only option. But even if I did that, could I do it with the rest of them? By myself? *Oh well*, I thought, *I'll just do one and deal with the rest later.*

I somehow managed to slide this one box down the ladder as planned, but not before it landed on the top of my head (yet another box falling on me), then dropped the rest of the way to the floor, spilling its contents out onto the hallway carpet. Yes, I know what you're thinking. Carpet in the hallway? Yes, but Evelyn and I had already discussed the fact that a realtor would probably insist we take it up to reveal the pristine hardwood floor beneath. At least we hoped it would be pristine. The whole house had been wall-to-wall carpeted since we'd lived there.

Anyway, that's what I was thinking about as I sat on the floor amid the spilled contents of the box, wondering how in the world I would get the rest of them down. I started to spread the pattern envelopes out in a fan shape in front of me to take a closer look at them.

I remembered that all but one of the patterns I'd found in the basement had been new, never used. According to Al, the ones I'd taken in to show him had all been from the late 1960s and early 1970s. He had explained to me the different styles, but that had meant very little to me at the time. From what I had learned from him since then, these looked to my untrained eye to all be from the 1960s – late in the decade if my budding style eye was right.

The first envelope I picked up was for a mini-skirted dress with those little puffed sleeves that seem to be coming back into style now. Interesting. And if it had been used – as its condition suggested it had – who had worn the dress? Certainly not my mother. It was so not her style.

I picked up another. The drawing on the front was of a smiling blonde woman wearing a tent-like jacket with a little stand collar – Asian influence perhaps – over slim pants. The illustration made it look as if the top might be made of brocade. The other smiling woman pictured was wearing a longer, coat-like version of the jacket that looked as if it might be made from quilted fabric. A bathrobe? Or housecoat as it was probably called back then? *Ooh*, I thought, *that would be comfy*! But it certainly didn't look like anything my mother would wear either, although, again, the pattern had clearly been used.

The third one really puzzled me. It was another tent-like dress pattern, but this one was marked "maternity." And it too had been used. *A 1960s maternity dress? WTF*? I shook my head. The back pocket of my now filthy jeans started vibrating. I slid my phone out to see a text from Karl.

"How u doing? Need any more help? Have a few hours today before our meeting."

I smiled. Perfect timing.

~

By the time I arrived at Miriam's house that evening – she was hosting again – Karl and I had managed to get all the boxes down from the attic, and they were now lining the hallway. I dared not take them any further through the house since they were so dirty. It seemed clear to both Karl and me that no one had been up in that attic since those boxes had been put in there, not even to look. I was puzzled about this. Why put stuff you never intend to use again in an attic? Why not just pitch it out? I would never understand the mind of a hoarder. But I couldn't bring myself to putting them in the trash without opening up every one of them to see what was there. What did that say about me? Evelyn would probably have an opinion.

So, there I was, showered and changed into clean jeans, sitting in Miriam's living room with a glass of wine and munching on cucumber slices slathered with cream cheese. She permitted mini-munchies before reading. More substantial eating was our reward for after.

“So, Charlie,” Miriam said as she threw the end of her voluminous red scarf over her shoulder, “no new dress this evening?” Was she smirking?

“As it happens, I do have a new one, Miriam, but I thought that it was a bit fancy for this evening’s gathering.” I think I batted my eyes.

“Well, in my experience,” she said as she heaved her considerable bulk into the love seat opposite me and very close to the nachos, “being over-dressed is preferable to being underdressed.”

I had no idea what she was talking about. She was always dressed in the same kind of outfit. The only thing that ever differed was the loudness of the pattern and the predominant colour. It seemed to me that she had a sort of uniform. I looked around at the rest of us in the room. Everyone had a uniform.

Karl, who was shuffling papers on his lap with one hand while balancing a beer with the other, was wearing his uniform: jeans, cowboy boots and a graphic T-shirt. Joseph, who was sitting in one of the wing-back chairs talking to Wendy who had managed to get here on time this evening, was wearing his uniform: dark, skinny jeans, a bit too short in my view, with a button-up shirt and a bow tie. Yes, a bow tie. He never wore the same shirt and tie combination two meetings in a row, but he always wore the same uniform. Even Wendy had that harried mom uniform: she was wearing yoga pants, sneakers and some kind of a tunic thing. She seemed to have a closet full of the same clothes. I wondered why everyone wore a uniform.

I took out my notebook and started making notes. Uniforms are easy. Uniforms give us a sense of the tribe we belong to. Uniforms are our armour. Uniforms tell the world who we are. Well, maybe they cover up what we really are. I'm not sure about that one. Anyway, it started me wondering about why I was trying on so many new ones. I was jolted out of my reverie by Miriam, who had begun reading from her latest project. It was some kind of weird dystopian romance, which is not at all up my alley, but we had all made a pact not to critique the genre itself. We couldn't all be expected to like historical mysteries, could we? That, of course, is my personal passion.

Miriam considered herself to be a talented creator of strange worlds where injustice has to be met by heroic righteousness and a well-endowed (*ahem*) male protagonist. My mind was wandering as it usually did when Miriam read, but she has impressive voice projection abilities, which she seemed to be projecting directly at me. Thus, I was awakened from my reverie state and brought back to the present moment with a start when she boomed, "You all do understand the post-apocalyptic world view I have conjured, I presume." It wasn't a question. It was more like a command.

Everyone was nodding, but their vacant expressions suggested to me that they were as much in the dark about her world as I was. And I can only presume that they had been listening. I had not.

"So, everyone, do you think that characters need to be known by their uniform?"

Miriam glared at me. "Am I finished?"

Karl smiled. "Great *non sequitur,* don't you think, though, Miriam?"

Miriam sat down. She always stood to read while the rest of us generally chose to read from a seated posture, sipping from our wine or beer as necessary.

"You were saying, Charlie?" Joseph said, opening his notebook. He seemed relieved to have had Miriam's performance cut short by my metaphorical hook.

I hadn't consciously planned to interrupt her, but my thoughts just seemed to take over. I had blurted before even thinking. *Oh well,* I thought, *let's dive in.* "Well, I was thinking about outward appearances of characters –"

"Oh, you must be talking about my characters Sapphire and Ruby," Miriam said, thumbing through her manuscript.

I hadn't been, but there you are. I continued. "I was thinking about how we all have uniforms. I mean, personally."

"I don't," Miriam said a bit haughtily, I thought.

Joseph looked down at what he was wearing that evening – which to my eye looked almost exactly like what he always wore. "I try not to wear anything that resembles any kind of uniform," he said.

"I understand how we all think about our own clothing choices and think that they're unique," I said, "but the fact is that we each have a kind of uniform that we wear in variations day after day. I'm not talking about school uniforms or police uniforms, although those also serve similar purposes."

"I'm not following." Wendy was usually very quiet during our discussions. This topic, though, seemed to have hit a nerve.

"I think I get it," Karl said. "Charlie has hit on something we can use for our characters. What we wear says a lot to the world, so what our characters wear, and their various variations on a single theme can let our readers know about deeper parts of their characters."

I smiled. At least Karl was getting it.

Joseph looked thoughtful. He was biting at the end of the ballpoint pen he always used to take notes during our meetings. "So, what you're saying is that a character's uniform doesn't necessarily mean that he's part of a group where they all wear the same uniform, are you?"

"It usually does mean that exactly, Joseph," I said. That didn't seem to sit well with the group.

Joseph continued his thought. "So, do you think that these clothing choices are prompted by something inside our characters or are they motivated by something outside them? Do they do it to be part of a group or just to always be the same?"

I thought about this a moment. Before I could get my thoughts together, Karl chimed in. "It depends," he said. "It's a question of locus of control."

Wendy looked up. She was frowning. It was clear she was just as puzzled as Joseph was, but I was trying to recall something I'd learned in a psychology class in university. But I now knew a thing or two about Karl, so I didn't interrupt him. He looked around as if to see if anyone else wanted to take over. There were no takers.

"I'm sure you all know what locus of control is even if the term itself isn't so familiar. It's a psychological construct coined by an American psychologist named Julian Rotter. In the '60s, he published a kind of scale to measure how much an individual's behaviour is influenced by internal factors versus external factors. Take, for example, two different people working in the same business. The one with the internal locus of control believes that success for her will be based on how hard she works and the overall effort she puts in.

On the other hand, her colleague with an external locus of control thinks that success is based on fate or some other uncontrollable factor like whether or not others like him. The one who believes he doesn't have control is likely to work less hard because he thinks it's pointless. As a result, he's likely to be less successful – kind of a self-fulfilling prophecy."

Joseph and Miriam both crossed their arms at almost the same moment. "I don't know," Joseph said. "There are lots of factors that are really out of our control. Take publishing, for example. A publisher can refuse to publish a book even if it's brilliant."

"Sure," Karl said, "but that's not the only factor, is it? If that publisher's decision makes a writer think that it's pointless to continue to write, and he stops, that guarantees his failure as a writer. That's an externally-controlled person. However, if that publisher's decision makes the writer double down on the work, then his chance of success is magnified." Karl took a sip of beer and sat back. "There are no guarantees in life in any case."

Who could argue with that? We continued our discussion about characters, and no one else actually had to read anything. I was relieved since what I'd brought to read was unformed, to say the least. Maybe next time.

I was still thinking about this the next day and trying to figure out if I was internally or externally focused when I walked through the door of *Sew Fine Things*. I could see two young women at the far end, looking at the silks. I knew they were looking at the silks because I now knew the location of almost every kind of fabric in this store that had become a kind of haven for me. They seemed to be arguing about something. They were checking their phones and feeling the fabric. Design students. I could tell by their uniform: some kind of neon hair colour, lots of piercings, funky clothes. At least they looked funky to me. *Yes*, I thought, *I do draw conclusions about people based on what they're wearing. So, sue me.*

"Charlie! How are you?"

Al's voice startled me out of my reverie. I turned. "Hello, Al. I'm great."

"Another dress this month, maybe?" He was smiling now as he walked behind the counter and made a note on a steno pad he always kept there.

"Well," I said, putting my backpack down on the counter. "I have a few more patterns here, but they all seem to be so out of my league, you know. My skills are still rudimentary, to say the least."

Al looked at me. "Okay, Charlie. What's really bugging you?"

How in the world did this man, someone I didn't know all that well, seem to know me? Although, to be honest, I had probably done a lot more talking in our now monthly encounters than he ever did. He probably did know quite a lot about me as he continued to listen patiently to me as I moaned about the work involved in clearing out a dead mother's house.

"How's the work going on the house?" he continued.

"I should be finished by now, but I can't quite seem to get my head around it."

"Are you sure you want it to be finished?"

"What? Of course."

Al shook his head ever so slightly and looked at me. No, strike that, he seemed to pierce me with his eyes. "What happens when the job is finished, Charlie?"

"I guess I have to sell the house." I stopped and listened to myself. "Then I have to move."

"Out or along?"

I had no earthly idea what he was talking about.

"'*The first and best victory is to conquer self*,'" he said. "Plato."

And suddenly I understood. I remembered that I had already conquered one thing. "Al," I said as I pulled last month's dress out of my backpack. "I think I managed to at least conquer the zipper thing."

He picked it up. "Charlie, I think you conquered your own fear of not being able to. Well done!" He looked at the dress carefully then folded it up so I could put it back in my backpack. "So, Charlie, let's see this month's patterns."

I retrieved my three choices from my backpack. As I pulled them out, a fourth tagged along and fell onto the counter. I picked it up and started to put it back into my bag. Al stopped me.

"Just a minute," he said. "Let's see that one."

I turned the envelope so that he could see the drawing. I hadn't looked at it very carefully. "Remember I told you that all the patterns I'd found in the basement were unused? All except one? This is the used one."

Al took it from me and looked closely at the picture on the front. It was what I would have called a "hippie dress" with its empire waistline and full-length skirt, long floaty sleeves caught at the wrists in a small cuff and ruffle around the neckline.

"Was this your mother's style?"

"Not at all," I said, taking it from him and looking at it. "Mom was kind of buttoned-down if you know what I mean. She was a tailored sweater and jacket kind of woman for all the years I knew her. But someone must have used it." I put it back in my backpack. I wondered if I might see a picture of someone wearing such a dress among Mom's old photos that I had yet to go through. I'd have to take a close look. I then spread out the three patterns I'd selected so that Al could see them. I had begun to think of him as my sewing guru.

He pointed at one with raglan sleeves and a funnel neckline. "This one," he said.

I was skeptical. It looked a bit complicated to me. "Al, I'm not sure –"

"This one," he said. "Remember what Plato said.

And so, I made that dress.

~

By the time the last day of May rolled around, I had almost completed the house clean-out. But I still had five cardboard boxes from the attic left and that duct-taped box that had been sitting in the basement since the day I had left it there. I had dragged it upstairs and put it on top of the pile of attic boxes in the hallway.

Tomorrow would be the first of June, and I really couldn't think of any more reasons why the house couldn't be ready to put on the market. Evelyn had already given me chapter and verse on why the beginning of the summer was the ideal time to list it with a realtor. I knew she was right. I also knew that

Al had been right. I had to conquer myself. I poured myself a glass of wine and got started on the boxes.

I had a box cutter that sliced slickly through the duct tape on the box I'd brought up from the basement. I sat cross-legged on the floor, took a sip of wine and pried off the cover. I'm not at all sure what I expected to find, but what I saw puzzled me. It was pieces of fabric. All the pieces were the same fabric, and I had no idea what they represented. I promised myself I'd figure it out.

June

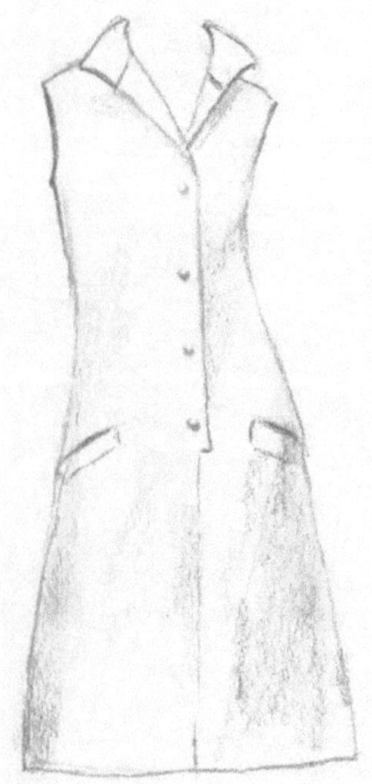

It was hard to believe, but the attic was now empty. I had gone through the contents of most of the boxes, and I could see the light at the end of the house-clearing tunnel. It was time to call Evelyn. The basement was relatively clean, the kitchen cupboards held only the essentials I needed to live, and the dining room had been cleared of all extraneous bits and pieces (except for the few bottles of liquor that remained. I mean, who actually drank crème de menthe? Yet, I could not bring myself to throw it out). There were, of course, still the boxes and sewing -related paraphernalia that I had stashed in the hall closet that I did not intend to show Evelyn at all.

I should have felt a major relief that the lion's share of this job was now behind me. What I felt was something more akin to melancholy. I was still trying to shake that feeling as I tapped on Evelyn's name on my phone. She answered on the first ring. I told her the house was ready for the next step. Her response didn't help to lift my gloominess in the slightest as she simply launched into the next phase.

"Call Tom Westhaver," she said. "Just a minute, I have to find his number in my contacts."

Evelyn and Tom had been in the same class in high school. I remembered that she had referred to him as the class nerd. He'd been the one with the thick glasses who knew more about computers than anyone else in the school, including the teacher who taught computer studies. I also remembered that Evelyn was convinced that he had a massive crush on her. That wasn't much of a stretch, though, since she'd been one of the "pretty girls" in high school. Not that she didn't also get good grades – she certainly did – and I had always wondered if Tom had been attracted more to her for her looks or her brains. Well, we'd never know since they'd gone to separate universities. He had eventually returned to his home town to sell real estate some years after his graduation. *Hmm*, I wondered, *why did she have his current contact information? And why in the world is brainy nerd Tom selling real estate?* I had expected him to own an internet company worth millions by now.

"Here it is," she said as she proceeded to give me his phone number and email address.

"So, Evelyn," I said, "you and Tom have been keeping in contact?"

"We're connected on LinkedIn. It seems his real estate career has taken off. At least for a small city, anyway. I doubt if he could make it here in Toronto. I messaged him a few weeks ago, so he's expecting your call."

"Why don't *you* call him?"

"I'm too busy to get into that. I have a new case that goes to court next week. You can look after this. Is there anything left in the house we need to deal with?"

We? I sighed. "No, Evelyn, nothing *we* have to deal with." She didn't seem to notice my sarcasm.

After I hung up, I looked down at the piece of paper with Tom's contact information. I decided to send him an email and give him my phone number. I wondered how soon he would call. Not too soon, I hoped. I still had some things I had to look after. The strange box that had fallen on me in the basement for one. I had taken only a cursory look at the pile of fabric it seemed to contain. It was now time to figure it out.

I had shoved the box into the back of the closet behind two others from the attic that I had yet to open. I figured they were probably all full of patterns, so there was no rush. I'd get to them. Eventually.

I pulled the two attic boxes out and set them aside. Then I took the peculiarly-shaped basement box out of the hall closet. I put it in the middle of the floor in the living room where there was some space to spread out. When I had first peeked inside it, I'd seen only that it seemed to be filled with pieces of fabric – pieces of fabric that all looked the same. It was time to work out its provenance and decide whether or not it should be kept or tossed.

I carefully removed the rest of the duct tape so that the fabric pieces didn't stick to them as I pulled them out then and sat back to see what I could make of it. Yes, t was stuffed with pieces of folded fabric – or at least that's what it looked like. I rifled through it a bit but still couldn't make heads nor tails of it. It was clear I'd have to take the fabric out and lay the contents on the floor so I could figure out what I was looking at.

I removed the first piece, unfolded it then laid it out flat on the floor. I smoothed it out. I stood up so that I could get a better view. My first impression was that there was a lot of fabric there. The piece itself was an odd shape, but even more peculiar was the material itself. It was white lace that had been backed with what looked and felt to me like white silk charmeuse. At this point in my fabric education, I knew what silk charmeuse felt like! But the backing seemed to have been sewn onto the individual piece of lace. I could see a row of sewing machine stitches all around the edges. The lace itself was an intricate geometric pattern. I sat down and took out another one. And another. I laid them all out on the floor then stood up again to look. Every piece was a different shape, or so it seemed, but every piece was the same in that they were all the same lace with the same silk backing sewn on. I just thought that it looked like a puzzle that had to be put together when it dawned on me. It was like a e*ureka!* moment.

My breathing started to come faster as I moved quickly to rearrange the pieces. This large one here, its mirror image there. This smaller piece here, its mirror image on the other side. I knew exactly what it was.

I was looking at pieces of fabric that someone had cut from a specific pattern and had begun sewing into a long white dress. *Oh my god*, I thought. *It's a wedding dress.* Or was it? And whose was it? It certainly wasn't Mom's, or did she perhaps abandon the idea of this one in favour of the sheath she wore in her wedding pictures when she and Dad married in the 1970s?

I stared at the pieces, squinted a bit and was able to figure out what the dress was supposed to look like. And it seemed familiar.

I ran into the kitchen where I had left my backpack. As I lifted out the patterns that were still there, I knew where I had seen this style before. It had been cut from the single used pattern I'd found in the basement boxes. It was a full-length, sort-of-but-not-quite-hippie-style dress. But since it had been cut from lace, it would be quite different in the end. There was no doubt about it. I could see the empire waistline, the puff of the long sleeves gathered at the wrists, the pieces that would make up the neckline ruffle. Yes, as I contemplated it, I was even more certain that it was a dress intended for a wedding – and it had been abandoned. I could feel a little tingle, just like the one I felt when I first uncovered the sewing machine in the basement. Maybe

Mom had been holding all of these things for someone. But who?

I didn't have time to think much more about this mystery since I had to get to work at the library. I carefully folded each piece and placed them all back in the box. It would have to contain its secrets for a bit longer. Duty called. Then, just as I was about to leave, Tom called.

I tried to hold the phone between my ear and my shoulder like they always do on TV when the characters are multi-tasking so that I could open, close and lock the side door behind me as we talked. I was not used to multi-tasking in even this small way. This was, without a doubt, a personal failing of mine – as Evelyn had so often expressed to me. To my credit, I dropped the phone only once during our conversation as I locked the door behind me and headed toward the library. Fortunately, it fell into a shrub – no damage.

Tom identified himself so formally that it occurred to me he probably didn't remember that he and I had met on several occasions when he was a senior in high school and I'd been a freshman. Why would he? He then expressed the requisite condolences on the "loss" of my mother before we got to the reason for the conversation.

"I understand from Evelyn that you two will be selling your family home. I'd be honoured to help you in any way I can."

Honoured? Geez, I thought, *realtors these days are one step up from used car salesmen.* At least that's how it looked to me, someone who had never had a single reason to deal with a realtor in my entire life.

We set up a meeting for the next day when he'd do a walk-through at the house, provide an evaluation of its market value and suggest how to "stage" it. It hadn't occurred to me that staging was a real thing, although Evelyn had used the word. Until that moment, I thought it was something those television real estate shows did for entertainment value. But I guess I was in for some kind of an education.

After we hung up, I found that I couldn't stop thinking about that box. It was just another part of the mystery of the sewing machine and the patterns. I would have to start making notes about it. By the time I walked through the automatic doors of the library, I was getting excited about the prospect that this could be the premise for a book. I might very well have my first really good book idea. As I pushed my book trolley around the stacks for the next three hours, I started to feel more and more excited. By the time I clocked out, there was an idea forming somewhere in the back of my brain, and it involved Sherlock Holmes.

~

Tom was nothing if not prompt. He arrived at the door precisely at ten o'clock the next morning. I was tapping mystery-related notes onto my laptop on the kitchen table and researching Sherlock Holmes's approach to solving mysteries when he arrived. I opened the door to find Tom Westhaver, high school nerd. Tom Westhaver, successful realtor. Tom Westhaver – gorgeous man? What the heck?

Tom stood on the front porch, briefcase in hand. He was wearing a pair of dark, skinny jeans with what looked to me like very expensive leather loafers, no socks. On top was a well-cut jacket over a paisley button-down shirt and a well-chosen tie. His heavy glasses were gone, and his hair was slightly longer than it had been in high school. He was still kind of short – only about five-eight – but he was still four inches taller than I am. I glanced over his shoulder and saw a black Tesla parked in front of the house.

He smiled and held out his hand while I stood there staring. "Charlotte. It's been a long time."

So, he did remember that we had met before. I ushered him into the house and offered him a cup of coffee. He accepted, and we sat down in the kitchen while he pulled out a portfolio he had prepared specially for me – us – this house.

"You know, you haven't changed a bit, Charlotte," he said as he slid the portfolio in my direction.

"Call me Charlie," I said, then added. "Everyone does."

He sat back and seemed to relax a bit. Up until that moment, I had felt a kind of tension, or perhaps just reserve. "Charlie. Yes, I remember Evelyn calling you Charlie back in high school. I wasn't sure you still liked the name."

"I guess I'll always be Charlie," I said. I wanted to say that he had changed, but I wasn't sure how to bring up the subject in a natural way. "You've certainly changed." Okay, so blurting is probably one way to do it, natural or not.

He laughed. "I suppose I have," he said, laughing lightly. "At least that's what everyone tells me." He pointed toward his eyes. "Lasik." He laughed.

"I have to ask," I said. "Why aren't you in computers or an internet business. You were brilliant."

"What makes you think I'm not?" He made a point of looking down at himself. "Oh, this. The wardrobe change. The truth is, Charlie, that I've always liked people more than machines. Don't get me wrong, I'm still that computer nerd. It's just now dressed up in a style that I'm able to afford these days." He stopped for one beat. "Now that I've sold my internet business. At a significant profit. But I still dabble."

I should have guessed. That explained a lot.

"So, shall we take a walk through the house?" He said, getting back to the matter at hand.

I nodded, and we began the tour. When we finished the circuit of the premises, we sat down at the kitchen table to discuss the details of putting the house on the market.

As he finished explaining to me the details of the contract that we would sign, he suddenly asked, "Are you married, Charlie?"

I couldn't imagine he didn't know the answer after having seen that I was living in the old family homestead. Alone.

I shook my head. "You?"

"Not yet," he said.

As we tidied up the paperwork, I decided to plunge right into a high school reminiscence. "You had quite a crush on Evelyn back in high school."

"Excuse me?"

"You know, she told me about it." I looked at his reaction and wasn't sure if it was utter disbelief or total embarrassment. I regretted it the moment it came out of my mouth.

"Do you really want to know the truth, Charlie?" he said as he packed his briefcase and began making his way toward the door. I wasn't at all sure I did, but I nodded anyway. "It wasn't Evelyn I had a crush on." He hesitated for just a moment. "It was you." He turned, walked out the door and closed it behind him.

~

I should have known that it was going to rain later that day. I heard the first clap of thunder just as I left the house, but I was so fixated on Tom as I got my things together to head downtown, I neglected to prepare. I suppose it's more correct to say that I was fixated on his revelation. I might even say stunning revelation since I was stunned. I was half a block from *Sew Fine Things* when it started to rain. Scratch that. It started to pour. I had forgotten my umbrella, so I was forced to sprint the rest of the way. I then literally fell into the shop tripping over my own feet as I tried to get inside before the next thunderclap, which was sure to increase the downpour. I caught myself just before I fell face-first into the floor, but not before I had twisted my ankle and had to grip the door handle to keep myself vertical.

Al looked up from where he was cutting a length of some kind of sparkly fabric for an older woman I'd not seen in the store before. My dramatic entrance caught her attention, and she looked up from where she had been concentrating on Al's always meticulous cutting. I expected some kind of scowl. Instead, her eyes widened, and she immediately came over to see if I was all right.

"Dear child," she said as she took my elbow. "Are you hurt?"

There was something vaguely familiar about her. I looked at her close-cropped, silver-coloured, pixie-style hair that reminded me of Dame Judi Dench. In fact, overall, she reminded me of DJD. It kind of made me feel giddy since I have always been a massive fan of Judi Dench's work. I remembered her in that British television show "As Time Goes By." Yes, this woman was a dead-ringer for the actress, although somewhat skinnier.

I tried to get up in as dignified a manner as I could. The woman was still holding my arm, and Al had returned to his fabric cutting. She looked at me closely. "Charlotte?" she said. "Charlotte Hudson?"

"Yes," I said, now genuinely puzzled. I looked at her again and realized that it was not Dame Judi that she reminded me of; instead, she reminded me of my old sewing teacher, Miss Davies. It suddenly dawned on me. It couldn't be, could it? This woman looked to be about Mom's age. Back in junior high when Miss Davies had taught me what was euphemistically called "Family and Consumer Studies," aka the early twenty-first-century version of home economics (an experience I mentioned before), I had thought she was at least seventy then. But, of course, when you're thirteen or fourteen years old, anyone over thirty is ancient.

Her face seemed to flood with recognition as she looked at me more closely. "It is you! When Al told me about the young woman who had started coming into his shop over the past few months, I had no idea it was you."

I had finally regained my composure – or at least as much as one can muster when one is dripping wet. "Miss Davies," I said when I finally caught my breath, "you haven't changed a bit!"

"How kind!" she said, not realizing that since I had thought her to be seventy back in junior high school, her age now would probably have been spot on. "On the other hand, Charlotte, you have, indeed, changed." She stopped and looked closely at me. "You look just like your mother did when she was around your age."

What? Miss Davies knew my mother when she was in her early thirties?

"Come see what I'm buying," she said as she moved back to the counter where Al was finishing folding up the third piece of fabric.

The little pile of neatly folded fabric was in various shades of blue. There seemed to be a large package of what looked like blue tulle like you might see in a ballerina's tutu, a plain blue that looked a bit like shiny jersey and the sparkly one he had been cutting when I made my grand entrance into the store.

"Wow," I said, "you must be making something very different from what you taught us to make back in junior high!"

"Indeed, I am," she said, picking up the piece of sparkly fabric. "Just picture this on a ballerina."

Uh-huh, just as I thought.

"I design and create costumes for *Pointe Taken Ballet Theatre*."

I had heard of the company. I wasn't much of a ballet fan myself, but did have fond memories of Mom taking Evelyn and me to see *The Nutcracker* in Toronto one year when we all tagged along with Dad on a business trip. I think I might have wanted to be a ballerina for a split second after that. However, given that I didn't have a musical bone in my body, it had been a non-starter. Evelyn, on the other hand, had taken ballet for years and had even been cast as one of several children in this very company's version of *Hansel and Gretel* when she was in high school.

As I touched the fabric, Miss Davies put her hand gently on top of mine. "I was so sorry to hear about your mother. I hadn't seen her in many years but had such fond memories of knowing her all those years ago. It always saddens me that we grow apart from so many people who have been a part of our lives."

I was mystified. I looked up at Miss Davies as Al moved away toward the back of the store as if he felt he had to leave us alone. "Miss Davies, I didn't know that you even knew my mother."

"Oh, yes," she said, her eyes sparkling and a small smile playing around the corners of her mouth. "I knew Kat Wilson very well." Just as fast as the sparkle had appeared, it evaporated.

Kat. I hadn't heard anyone refer to Mom as Kat in many years. Dad had bristled every time he heard someone refer to her that way, which wasn't often. To him and everyone else, she was Katherine. Katherine with the perfect lipstick, the button-down shirts, the Brooks Brothers cardigans, even the pearls every so often. Kat always seemed to refer to a different person.

"Miss Davies, did Mom ever sew?"

It was her turn to look mystified. "But of course, Charlotte. I'm surprised you didn't know this."

I shook my head. "I was wondering," I started, not knowing if it was appropriate to broach the subject. I noticed Al returning to the counter with two bolts of what I recognized as seersucker fabric – one with red and white stripes, the other in blue and white stripes – which he put down on the end as Miss Davies got her credit card out of her handbag. "I was wondering if you knew if Mom ever made a wedding gown."

A cloud seemed to flit over her eyes for a split second. At least that's what I thought I saw. "Goodness, Charlotte," she said, looking at her watch as Al handed her the receipt. "Look at the time. It's been wonderful to run into you. I do hope we'll connect again. I must be off." She put her handbag over her shoulder as Al handed her the bag. She blew him a kiss, smiled at me and fled.

"Hello, Charlie," he said. "Nice to see you!"

"Nice to see you, Al," I said as I distractedly looked at Miss Davies's back disappearing across the street, her umbrella shielding her from the downpour. "Al, does Miss Davies shop here often?"

"One of my best customers," he said, pulling the two bolts off fabric from the end of the counter so that they were now right in front of me. "Charlie, I thought of you when these came in. All we need now is a pattern!"

I pulled three of the unused ones I'd retrieved from basement boxes out of my backpack. These three had caught my eye as dresses I could actually wear this summer. Two of them looked a lot like the one I had made last month, so I really liked those. The third one, I was almost hesitant to show Al. If I knew him, he'd probably want me to make that one. But if I'm being honest, it was the one I liked the most.

Just as I feared, Al picked up the third one and turned over the envelope to read the back. "This one."

"Oh, god, Al. It has buttonholes." The dress was a chic sleeveless sheath with a collar that was popped up and a button placket that started at the collar and ended just above the waist. "I can't make that. I have no idea whatsoever about how to put together a collar. And I don't even know if Junior makes buttonholes."

"Junior?"

"Charlie Junior. My sewing machine. I named her."

He laughed. "Well, I guarantee you that Junior can make buttonholes," he said. "You *can* do this, you know."

"I don't know, Al. I think I might have maxed out in the sewing skill thing. I mean, I want to. I do love the style of this dress, but I don't think I can."

Al looked at me in that way he has. "'*If you hear a voice within you say 'you cannot paint' then by all means paint, and the voice will be silenced.'* Van Gogh knew it worked for painters. I know it will work for you. It just takes a bit of self-discipline, Charlie. And you know it."

Of course, he was right.

"So, you know Miss Davies?" he said, still holding the pattern.

"She was the person who taught me to sew."

"I thought she might have been."

"What I didn't know was that she knew my mother. And if my mother knew how to sew, why didn't she ever mention it to her daughters?"

I then went on to tell Al about the puzzling wedding dress pieces I'd found. When I was finished, he whistled softly. "That's quite a find, Charlie. What do you suppose it means?"

"That's just it. I have no idea. I don't even know if it was my mother's project at all. But why would she start something like that then abandon it? Why would anyone? And what about Miss Davies? When I had Miss Davies as a teacher, why didn't Mom ever mention to me that they knew one another?"

"*'If you cannot get rid of the family skeleton, you may as well make it dance.'*"

I looked at Al and waited.

"George Bernard Shaw," he said.

Of course, it was. And I knew I'd have to figure out a way to make the skeleton dance.

July

When the email ping sounded, I had almost forgotten about my room-mates and the fact that they had sub-let my room.

"Hey, Charlie...hope the clean-out stuff is going well. Big news. Landlord sold the house, and we all have to move out. I found a box of your things in the front hall closet. Let us know when you can pick it up. Arch."

How could I have forgotten about the fact that I still needed a place to live when the house sold? The email kind of knocked the wind out of my sails. I had finished that chic, sleeveless, seersucker dress and had even managed to make respectable buttonholes. But now I had a real problem.

Where in the world *was* I going to live? And perhaps, even more important, how was I going to pay for it? I supposed that there might be a bit of money coming to me from the house sale, but it would take some time for that to be available. And the truth was that I harboured a secret hope that any money I saw from my share of the house proceeds might go in an investment account toward my own house someday. Of course, I would have preferred going down that path with a significant other, but I wasn't averse to the idea of going it alone. I wondered what Evelyn and Michael would do with theirs. Perhaps they'd sell the condo and buy a house? Not likely. They lived for work, and they'd have to spend hours every day commuting if they went that route.

I was still thinking about this an hour later when I realized that Tom would be arriving any time now to help me make some decisions about the house staging. I wondered if he might have any insights into rental real estate.

I looked down at the ratty black shorts I'd had for years by way of Old Navy and the T-shirt that was a size (or two) too small for me and decided that this would not do. I had to look a bit more professional if I was "taking" a meeting with a realtor – and his stager, whoever that might be.

I opened the front hall closet, which was where I was temporarily stashing my newly-created dresses. I pulled out the closest one. It was the seersucker that I'd just finished. It had been a bit of a bitch to say the least. I hadn't been too far off the mark about my ability to make a collar when Al had encouraged me to do it. I had tuned into my YouTube sewing guru once again, and Grace, my sewing whisperer, did not fail me. I put my iPad on a dining room chair that I'd pulled in beside the sewing machine, then I started and stopped her video a dozen times while I sewed. This was after watching it about a hundred times before I dared proceed. In the end, I'd nailed it. And those respectable buttonholes? Al was right. Junior did have a gizmo that did them all by itself! I had, however, taken his advice and done at least a dozen test ones first. I was pretty proud of the work. Anyway, it was blue and white striped seersucker and was just about perfect for a hot July day. I had forgotten that Mom and Dad never had gotten around to retrofitting the house with air conditioning.

Just as he had done on the first visit, Tom rang the doorbell precisely on time. When I opened the door to find him, briefcase in hand again, standing on the front steps, I was nearly speechless. Was it possible he was even more handsome in his summer blue-and-white-striped seersucker jacket and white jeans? Or, perhaps it was because we looked like long-lost twins? The look on his face suggested he was wondering the same thing – the long-lost twin thing, I mean.

We both looked down at our own clothing and started to laugh.

"Fantastic dress, Charlie!" Tom said as soon as he stopped laughing.

"Thanks! Fantastic jacket!" I said. "You know, I made this dress myself." I did a little twirl.

"Really? I didn't know that you were creative." He looked a bit flustered. "What I meant to say is that I know you're creative – after all, you are a writer. I just didn't know that you were –"

I put him out of his misery. "I know what you mean. Not to worry! You are now a member of a very select group – people who know I can sew!"

He bowed just slightly. "I am honoured."

I glanced behind him as he came into the house past me. "Where's your stager person?"

"Lucinda? Late as usual."

Tom and I settled in at the kitchen table with fresh cups of coffee. I had broken down and bought some more Nespresso™ capsules, so I was treating the two of us to something a step up from my usual instant swill. It felt so grown-up. We were chatting about the general state of the local real estate market when we heard a car door slam shut out front. Tom got up and went to the living room window that looked out into the front yard and the street beyond. "It's Lucinda," he said as he made his way to the small front foyer to open the door for her. "Here she comes, bag and baggage. I hope you're ready for this."

I had no idea what he was talking about. Then he opened the door, and a typhoon blew in. There was Lucinda – a twenty-something ball of palpable energy. She had a large shoulder bag over one shoulder, an enormous camera slung over the other one. She was carrying a portfolio as big as a full piece of Bristol board and was managing to balance her phone between her right shoulder and her ear, a talent we all know I had yet to perfect.

She was breathless, no doubt from trying desperately to be on time. She finished her telephone conversation, dropped her portfolio on the floor, let the shoulder bag drop to a nearby chair and stuck out her hand. "You must be Charlie," she said her bright green eyes (were those coloured contacts?) smiling as widely as her perfectly aligned, astoundingly white teeth. She reminded me of an actress in a recent toothpaste commercial on television whose bizarrely white teeth practically hurt your eyeballs if you looked at them too long.

I nodded and shook her hand. Lucinda was nothing if not dazzling. Even her long, loose blonde hair dazzled. I glanced over at Tom. Was he smirking? He shrugged just slightly.

After we had exchanged very few pleasantries, Lucinda began taking equipment out of the shoulder bag as if she were Mary Poppins. I was amazed at how much gear she had stashed inside. She laid it all out on the coffee table and picked up an iPad, a measuring tape and a stylus. Then slinging the camera around her neck, she looked around. "Mind if I poke around by myself? I do my best creating when I'm alone."

I had no problem, but creating? Who was she kidding? She was here to throw in a few new glass-topped tables and mirrored bedside tables if the television real estate shows were to be believed. I'd been looking at a few as research for this very moment.

"So...what's with all her gear?" I said to Tom when she was out of earshot.

He started to laugh. "Oh, Lucinda takes her job very seriously. She graduated from an online interior decorating course a few months ago and fancies herself a bit of an artist."

"And she already has her own staging business?"

"Oh, that," Tom said, sitting back down at the kitchen table. "Did I mention that she's my niece? And I owe my brother a favour? He bankrolled her, so it's kind of important to him that she succeeds. She's actually quite good at this. I'm sure you understand."

I did understand.

"One thing we can be sure of," he said, sipping his coffee, "is that the staging will be overdone rather than underdone."

He was undoubtedly right about that. When Lucinda had returned from her solitary fact-finding mission (which didn't take long given the small size of the bungalow), she was full of ideas. The first and foremost one in her mind was the one that Evelyn and I had discussed and that I dreaded – she insisted that we had to pull up every single piece of wall-to-wall carpet. It was outside my realm of experience to try to understand why someone who buys the house couldn't do this if we just charged them less.

"Charlie," she said, "that's just not how it works. We need to create a beautiful canvas so that potential buyers can see themselves in the space. No, not see, so much as feel." She closed her eyes, evidently in some kind of ecstasy at this thought.

Tom stifled a grin. I looked at him and could feel an eruption of laughter overcoming me. I tried to stop it. Then he started. Then I couldn't stop.

Lucinda opened her eyes and looked from me to Tom and back. "What's so funny?"

"Oh," I said, trying to stifle yet more peels of laugher, "we were just talking about something funny that happened when we were in high school."

"Oh, of course," she said. "I remember my father telling me that you two went to high school together. Wow, that was a long time ago, huh?"

We were only ten or twelve years older than she was. So, it wasn't like we were ready to hit the retirement homes any time soon. The thought, though, was enough to sober us both up.

By the time Lucinda packed up and left, I had a list as long as my arm of things that had to be done. By me. Despite all the work I'd done to date, Lucinda wanted the house essentially cleared out. I mean, she wanted me to get rid of furniture or at least store it somewhere, possibly the basement. However, I was adamant that my bedroom had to stay as did Evelyn's, although hers would be clear of everything except her bed, a bedside table and a lamp.

"That red table and chairs can stay in the kitchen," she said. "It adds a bit of a mid-century-modern vibe. It's all the rage these days," she said.

As for the rest, Lucinda would add the "fluff." Then, I had to bring in the interior painters and change the hardware on all the kitchen cupboards (she would send along the replacements she would select). I had to have the carpets removed and trashed and then have the hardwood floors refinished (after she had viewed their condition) if she deemed them to be in too rough shape. I sincerely hoped they would not need refinishing. In any event, I had to have the place professionally cleaned and prepped, then she would send in her assistants with furniture and "artwork." I was just considering how much all of this was going to cost when Tom, as if reading my mind, offered, "I know this sounds expensive, Charlie, but trust me, the selling price will be higher, and it's likely to sell faster."

I was slightly mollified but was quite daunted by the work still ahead. I really was going to have to get through all those old photographs...and soon.

"I'll give you a call in a day or two to see how things are going," Tom said as he left.

I looked down at the handful of business cards he and Lucinda had left – painters, landscapers, trash removers (I didn't need this one, I had my own contacts in that business!). I guess I'd have to start making phone calls. The first one would be to Evelyn to give her the update.

~

By the time I had gotten off the phone with Evelyn, I was in need of a drink. Since I had a writing group meeting this evening – Joseph was hosting again – I poured myself only a half glass of wine and sipped it as I got ready. Would I wear one of my dresses this evening? Maybe not.

Evelyn had been less than excited about the fact that this "staging" was likely to result in yet a longer delay in the house sale. However, she did suggest that I let her know when it was ready so that she could consider coming to see it once again before it was sold. I had never suspected that my sister was the nostalgic type, but perhaps she just wanted to protect her investment, so to speak. As I thought about our conversation, I poured myself another half glass of wine and drank it rather more quickly than I was used to because I was going to be late if I didn't leave right away.

When Joseph let me into his flat half an hour later, I was surprised to find that Wendy had managed to arrive before I did. This was the second time in three months that she'd been here on time. I wondered what was up with her. Even Karl and Miriam were not there yet.

"Fabulous tie, Joseph," I said as he waved two bottles of wine at me – one red, one white – so that I could make a choice. I pointed in the general direction of the white. This evening's bow tie was some kind of red, green and yellow tartan as far as I could make out. "Are you writing something Scottish?" Joseph's ties almost always signified something related to his writing.

"Ah, Charlie. There's where you need a bit of an education." He adjusted the bow slightly. "This, my dear, is an Irish tartan."

Up until that very moment, I had no idea that Ireland was a land of tartans. I had always associated them with Scotland.

"It is the tartan of County Galway. And yes, I am writing something that is partially set in the Galway area of Ireland."

"Have you visited there?" Wendy said.

"Not in person, but I have done a lot of online research."

"Haven't you always said that you had to experience things to be a real writer?" Wendy said, making what I considered to be an excellent point. Joseph had often spoken (at length) about the need for writers to have varied life experiences.

Before Joseph could answer, Karl and Miriam arrived together. While they were doing the usual greetings and drink orders in the foyer, I thought it might be nice to strike up a conversation with Wendy. Of all the people in the group, I knew her the least. And this evening, the perpetually harried mother of three seemed subdued.

"So, Wendy, how's the writing going?"

"Oh, you know. It's hard with the kids around, but I think I'm starting to make some progress." Her voice was low and slow. She seemed to have slowed down so much as to be half asleep.

"What are you working on?" I tried to see her eyes clearly, but she wore large, black-rimmed glasses that covered half her face. It had occurred to me that she might be on something.

"Oh, it's a new children's picture book, and I'm trying my hand at illustration." She leaned toward the plate of biscuits on the table. "Have you tried these?" she said, smiling languidly as she took a big bite out of what looked like Joseph's famous savoury shortbreads. And then I knew.

"Wendy, you might want to go a little easy on those," I said, trying to pry it out of her fingers. "You know that Joseph adds a little something to his biscuits." By "a little something," I meant that he was an expert with the cannabis butter. It was abundantly clear that Wendy had probably already consumed her quota.

"Oh, yes," she said, giggling like one of her children might. "You're probably right!"

Miriam, Karl and Joseph finally had their drinks in hand, we had our greetings out of the way and were all settled in our respective chairs.

"I'll begin this evening," Joseph said, perching his reading glasses – which were more for show than anything else since he wasn't really old enough to need them in my view – on the end of his nose. Joseph began with his Irish tale that seemed to involve some kind of time-travelling leprechaun. Or something. My mind was wandering.

"Well, that was very creative," Miriam opined when he had finished. "I did like the leprechaun bits, but I wonder if you might not be able to come up with a more plausible storyline."

"I believe that the words leprechaun and plausible cannot really be put in the same sentence," Joseph said.

Was that a sniff I heard from Miriam? Joseph continued. “I have taken a creative approach to reality.”

“What does that mean?” Miriam sipped her wine and re-crossed her arms across her ample breasts that were this evening swathed in what appeared to be a red chiffon caftan of some kind.

“Well, Miriam,” Joseph began – I could tell from his tone of voice that he was preparing for a sparring match. I woke up and paid attention. These altercations were always the highlight of any group meeting. “I believe your continuing focus on plausibility, believability, credibility, whatever it might be called, stifles the creativity that writing these days so desperately needs.”

“Are you suggesting that my writing is not the product of intense creativity?”

Joseph shrugged.

Miriam turned to Karl. “What do you think?”

Karl looked as if he might be searching for an escape route. He looked at me then back to Miriam. “I think that creativity manifests itself in many different approaches,” he said slowly as if choosing his words very carefully. He sounded a bit like a politician.

Of course, his generic answer was not going to satisfy Miriam. “Creativity manifests itself? What kind of B-S is that?”

"I think creativity means using your imagination," Wendy said. Everyone looked at her. She wasn't usually given to expressing opinions of any sort. "I mean, when something doesn't seem creative, isn't it really because it lacks imagination?"

I could go along with that. Then I added, "I agree with Wendy. But I do kind of disagree with Joseph. I do think that believable stories can be very creative. I mean, isn't it just a matter of looking at that believable story in a new and imaginative way? Of not being derivative of the work of others?"

Everyone except Joseph was nodding. "What," he said, "do you think is the most creative art form?" He seemed to want to change the subject slightly.

That was a tough one. Miriam said, "Literature has long been considered the highest form of art."

"Is highest the same as most creative? I've often read that painting is the highest art form," Karl said as he took a healthy swig of his beer. "But I guess in the end, it's just a matter of opinion."

"I think it depends on the kind of imagination that goes into it," Wendy said. "I think that my illustrations are very imaginative. If I copied someone else's work, they might look the same, but they wouldn't be creative at all."

"Well, I personally believe that creative work comes from those of us who live a creative life," Miriam said, pouring herself another glass of wine.

"What exactly *is* a 'creative life,' Miriam?" Karl asked. Joseph leaned in as if to await her answer with bated breath.

"It is a way of being," she said, readjusting the scarf-like contraption that was beginning to sag down toward her ample midsection. "It is a way of seeing the world. It is a life of constant curiosity, of following the wind and not bowing to convention."

"I think that might more properly be labelled an unconventional life," Karl said. He gave her a slight lop-sided smile, clearly revelling in baiting her just a bit.

"Perhaps it does suggest unconventionality. However, that is, in my view, a prerequisite for creativity."

"I live a pretty conventional life," Wendy said quietly.

Miriam sniffed but said nothing.

"As do I, Wendy," Karl said. He turned back to Miriam. "You know, Miriam, I think you may have missed the point of the creative life. It's not really about conventionality or how you dress or how you think about the world. You've forgotten something important.

'*To live a creative life, we must lose our fear of being wrong.*"

"Joseph Chilton Pearce," Joseph said. "*The Magical Child*?"

"Not sure which of his books it came from, but Pearce said it." Karl looked at Miriam. "Do you still fear being wrong?"

My head was starting to hurt. It might have been the wine, but it was just as likely to be the conversation. It was patently obvious none of us knew what we were talking about. But that was nothing new for a group of writers.

~

By the time the third week in July rolled around, I'd already begun the work Lucinda had instructed me to have done. The carpet-remover guys had been in and had removed wall-to-wall carpeting from every inch of the house and, just as we had hoped, the floors they revealed beneath were pristine hardwood that needed only a slight buffing to make them gleam. The painters had just left, and I could smell the lingering scent of fresh paint. Lucinda had also been right about the colour. Even with the old furniture still in place, the house looked bigger and more cohesive with its neutral colour palette. *This*, I thought, *is what creativity is all about. Making a silk purse out of a sow's ear.* Lucinda had been right about her creativity.

When all the workers had finally left, I could make a trip to *Sew Fine Things*. I had three new patterns to show Al and was excited to begin a new project.

There were three other customers in the store when I arrived, so I was left to my own devices to search through the bolts of fabric. I had begun studying up on the internet about fabric types and found that I was now able to understand what it meant when the label said "polyester, rayon and spandex" or "cotton, linen and lycra."

My hand came to rest on a bolt of white linen with a subtle slub texture. I lifted an edge of the fabric and scrunched it in my hand. I was looking at the wrinkles when Al found me down a long aisle piled to the ceiling on either side with bolts of fabric. "It wrinkles expensively," he said, smiling.

"I noticed. I love it, wrinkles and all. I think this is the one I want today."

"Yes, Ma'am," he said with a little salute as he slid the bolt carefully out from its spot on the shelf. "So, what are we making today?" he said as he placed the bolt on the cutting counter. "By the way, I see that you were able to conquer your fears last month. The dress looks smashing."

I was uncommonly tickled that he had noticed I was wearing the seersucker dress. I was, indeed, quite proud of it. I did a little twirl. He smiled and nodded. "Well done, Charlie. So, what will you be making with this beautiful fabric?"

I took three patterns out of my backpack. I know – a backpack isn't a good look with a summer dress – but you have to admit it's practical. I fanned them out on the counter.

Al looked carefully at each one in turn. He then touched the fabric as if it could tell him which one would be best. "This one," he said, pointing to one of the envelopes.

I picked up the pattern and looked thoughtfully at the drawing. It was an A-line dress (as were most of the dresses from its vintage) with what they call princess seams – a seam that ran from each armhole to the hem to give it shape – and some kind of a bow at the front split of the funnel neck. I wasn't at all sure I liked that bow. But I was determined to open my style mind.

"Okay," I said. "I think I might be able to accomplish this one."

"That's what I like to hear from my customers!"

"Al, do you think that sewing is a craft or a kind of art?"

“Of course, it’s art. It’s an art because of what you put into it.”

“Okay, I’ll bite. What do I put into it that makes it art?

“*Art is not a handicraft, it is the transmission of feeling the artist has experienced.*”

“Who said that?”

“Leo Tolstoy,” he said. And so, Tolstoy had the last word. I’d have to convey this to my writer’s group. I could hardly wait.

~

Lucinda arrived to do a walk-through of the work that had been accomplished to date, and she was reasonably happy. But she chided me that I’d have to live very carefully in my room after the staging furniture was delivered. It was scheduled for two days hence. Before she left, she turned to the three large cardboard boxes that I had removed from the closet and left in the hallway outside my bedroom. She pointed. “Those have to go.” She looked at me, and I could see the light dancing off her crystal earrings. “I mean it, Charlie,” she said as she picked up her handbag to leave. I knew she meant it.

The boxes were the last three of Mom's attic stuff. Every time I looked at them and considered opening them, I think I realized that I'd be letting go of the very last parts of Mom—and maybe even Dad. I couldn't be sure unless I opened them.

One was marked photos, and judging from how heavy it was, the job of reviewing and sorting them would likely be onerous. One of the other two was labelled photo albums – another heavy one – but at least I could expect those photos to be somewhat organized. The third was labelled "Papers." Cryptic, to say the least.

I carried – or rather pushed – the box into the living room, made myself a martini (I do have to admit mine were not quite as good as Evelyn's), plopped three olives into my glass and settled in on the floor to go through the photos.

When I opened the box, I groaned. It was full of loose photos just as I had feared. As I pulled out the first handful, I noticed that some of them were very old, indeed. They must have been a hundred years old judging from the attire and the poses. Were they of my ancestors? Probably. It struck me. I could try to catalogue them according to the type of dress and figure out – with the help of Mr. Google – the eras. I could learn about fashion throughout the twentieth century. Maybe I could even write something about it. I was suddenly invigorated. I'd need some way to keep them organized, but that could wait until tomorrow. This evening, I would create piles on the floor, each one signifying a decade – if the decades were all represented.

I'd been at this pursuit for two hours and two martinis, and I had yet to see a single face that looked even remotely familiar. I looked in the box and decided to call it a night. *Just one more handful*, I thought.

I yawned as I dealt each one like a pack of cards. I stopped at the fifth one. I was drawn to a face that looked vaguely familiar. But it wasn't the face that drew me further into it. It was the dress the young woman was wearing. It fell almost to her ankles with full, bell-shaped sleeves and an empire waist where small gathers fell from right below the bust. It was clearly made from some kind of lightweight material – cotton perhaps – since it was blowing in the breeze. I could almost see it undulating. It was covered with tiny flowers. She was barefoot and had a small crown of flowers on top of her flowing, wavy hair. The young woman was leaning against a scruffy-looking young man who sported a beard, a pair of low-slung jeans and nothing else. He was looking at her with rapture in his eyes. I felt a tingle up the back of my neck.

I stared at the photo. Where had I seen that dress before? Then it struck me. It was pictured on one of the pattern envelopes I had found in the attic. I had placed all the used patterns from the attic in a large plastic bin

I'd bought (I had bought a half a dozen) at *Canadian Tire.* The containers were now residing in my bedroom closet. I got up, staggered just a tiny bit and went to the bin to see if I could find it. Bingo! It was near the top of the first bin.

I returned to the living room and sat down, staring first at the photo, then at the pattern envelope and back again. There was no doubt about it. The dress was the same one – and the pattern had, indeed, been used. So, now I focused on the faces.

There was now no doubt in my mind whatsoever. It was my mother. I flipped the photo over and was rewarded by a scrawl on the back. I didn't recognize the handwriting. It said, "Woodstock, 1969," and there was a tiny heart. I turned the photo over and concentrated on the young man's face. Nothing. It certainly wasn't. Dad.

August

Three days later, I was lying awake in bed at six a.m. staring at the ceiling. The photo had been haunting me. I hadn't been able to get the image out of my head. All I could see was my mother at Woodstock, of all places, in a hippie-style dress with a man I had never seen in my life, or ever heard mentioned. And there she was, looking happier and more carefree than I had ever seen her. Who was this person I'd called Mom for thirty-two years? And Woodstock? Please. My mother had spent her entire adult life as a conventional, buttoned-down substitute high school English and History teacher married to an accountant living in the suburbs with two young daughters. I was beginning to think that my mother must have a long-lost twin sister. Wait a minute...

I contemplated discussing it with Evelyn, but I wasn't ready for that yet. I wasn't ready for her initial horror then her adamant insistence that it wasn't Mom anyway. I was sure that this would be her position on the matter. It was just who she was. And, besides, this was probably a discussion to have in person rather than over the phone. Eventually. The truth is that Evelyn had seemed very peculiar on the phone lately whenever she checked in to see how the house sale was going. She always seemed as if she wasn't really "in" the conversation. She seemed distant, far away. Anyway, yes, the house sale.

One of the other reasons I was wide awake so early was that the first three house showings were scheduled for today. I would have to spend an hour or more getting the place spotless then make myself scarce for the rest of the day. Tom was bringing one potential buyer this morning, a young couple with two children he had told me, then two other realtors had also made appointments with their own clients one after the other for the afternoon. Since I had to work at the library for a couple of hours today, I'd only really need to find somewhere to perch for about two hours. It had only been a week since I'd finished making the white linen dress, but I was itching to get into another project. The fabric shop seemed like a good option, but I had other matters to attend to. There was the little matter of finding somewhere to live. I would get to that.

I showered, ate breakfast, tidied and vacuumed. As Lucinda had suggested, I had dumped all my clothes as well as the boxes that I was still sorting/keeping in Mom and Dad's walk-in closet. I would lock it, and the potential buyers would have to be content with the photo of the space that I was planning to affix to the double doors of the closet. As I put away the last of the boxes, I remembered when Mom and Dad had done the renovations to this old house. The house was built some years before ensuite bathrooms and massive walk-in closets were *de rigeur*. That was the time before life didn't seem worth living without them. At least in North America.

Mom had planned it all. Dad never had a chance. The house had four bedrooms, although one of them could hardly be called a bedroom these days. It was smallish and had only one tiny window. But it did have a closet (which is what made it a bedroom according to the real estate people). I suppose it might have been planned by the architect to be a nursery since it was right next to the master bedroom, but Mom had only ever used it as an extension of her closet anyway. No one except Mom ever went in there. As I remembered this, it occurred to me that she might have stashed her sewing machine in there before it ended up in the basement, but now, I'd never get a chance to ask her about it.

She drew out the plans for the renovation, after which Mom and Dad became the first homeowners on the street to have both an ensuite bathroom and a walk-in closet. Of course, over the years, most of the other houses on the street had been renovated and enlarged beyond what anyone could ever have envisioned in their wildest imaginations in the late 1970s when they had originally bought their houses. Just next door, the one-time bungalow was now a monstrous two-story behemoth with a family room extension out the back that took up three-quarters of the back yard. I only hoped that the smallish nature of our little rancher wouldn't be too off-putting to a young couple.

After I'd finished prepping the house, I donned my newest summer dress – the white linen one – hot off the sewing machine and walked around the place. It no longer looked like the family home where Evelyn and I grew up. It looked more like those slightly upscale, bland houses of indeterminate style that you see on real estate listings. In a word, it looked *staged*. Because, of course, it was.

The living room was kitted out with two grey couches that had matching but artfully placed toss cushions. The cushions were yellow, black and grey, providing what Lucinda had called a "pop of colour." The square wood coffee table with its handy drawers and bottom shelf had been replaced by a round one with a glass top and what appeared to be brass underpinnings. It looked considerably more precious and less functional than the one I'd known and loved for years. Oh yes, and a taupe and cream area rug was pulling it all together. I wasn't at all certain what kind of people could picture themselves here. It would probably be Evelyn's friends from what I remembered from having met a few. I only hoped Lucinda knew what she was doing.

I checked my watch. Tom would be here with his potential buyers in fifteen minutes. I knew I had better get going. Before I hit the fabric store, though, I did have a more pressing task to complete. I had made appointments to see two apartments today. How I was going to pay the rent was another story for another moment of panic. I'd have to come up with something to show a landlord that I was good for it. I wasn't sure that a payslip from a twenty-hour-a-week job would be enough. Right now, though, I just hoped I looked like the kind of tenant one of them would want because if Tom was successful in his pursuit of a buyer, I'd be homeless.

The first apartment was slightly farther out of town than even my suburban family home, so I took a bus that wended its way toward a new area of multiple apartment buildings. On the way, I examined my fellow passengers as I liked to do. There were several teenagers mostly staring bleary-eyed into their phones. There were also quite a few older people who looked so tired they made me want to yawn.

When I arrived at my stop, two older women and one frail older man got off just in front of me. As the bus pulled away, I stopped to check the directions on my phone and noticed the three of them trudging up a hill toward what looked like it was probably a kind of retirement home. You know the ones. They are usually under four stories high – this one was three – and then generally sprawl out in long corridors. There is also a canopy over the front door and lots of cars in the parking lot, presumably more for staff and visitors than for the inhabitants. My phone told me that I should proceed in the opposite direction, so I did.

Five minutes later, I was standing in front of an unprepossessing six-story building. The stucco facing was dotted with tiny balconies. I stood for a moment looking at the front door. It was one of those sliding ones like they have at the entrance into a subway station. My first thought was that everything looked clean enough, but there was something about the place that didn't speak to me. At least, what it seemed to be saying to me wasn't altogether encouraging. I couldn't shake the feeling that I was a fish out of water here, but I didn't know why. I buzzed the superintendent then waited.

A few minutes later, a man I judged to be in his late fifties or early sixties arrived to open the door for me. He was wearing a T-shirt with some kind of a brewery logo that stretched across his rather ample mid-section. He had a pair of what looked like Rayban™ sunglasses pushed up on his forehead below a shiny bald head. When he smiled, he had a space between his front teeth, making him look just a bit creepy.

"Hi there," he said. "You must be Charlotte." Did his eyes actually flit over me from head to toe and back?

I nodded, and he let me in. "Only got one unit available today," he said as he pushed the button to summon the elevator. "It's on the fourth floor." He smiled. I could feel him watching me as I got in the elevator with him. "I'm sure it's just what you're looking for."

I was hopeful – but not for long.

Gerald – his name was Gerald – unlocked the door to unit number 405. As soon as he opened the door, I was assailed with a smell that resembled curry mixed with cat pee. I almost gagged.

"Sorry about the smell," he said. "It kind of lingers in the carpets, but everyone gets used to it."

I had no desire to see anything else once I noted that the carpets to which he referred were wall-to-wall green shag rugs right out of the 1970s. They were in worse shape than the ones that the carpet-removers had hauled off to the dump from my mother's house just two weeks earlier. And while I'm on the topic of dumps, I was looking at one. The outside of the place might have been clean, but as Gerald and I had moved from the front door into the elevator and into the fourth-floor corridor, I noted a trend. Everything became increasingly poorly maintained and grimy. I tried to back out the door, but Gerald was blocking my way. "Let me show you the rest of the apartment." He smiled again, and I wanted to run.

He moved toward the kitchen. I preferred to stay as close to the door as I could. Since the apartment was small, he didn't have to move very far to point out the living room, the bedroom and the bathroom. "You probably want a few minutes to look around by yourself," he said finally.

"No," I said, trying to smile. "No, I think you've done a great job. I've seen enough... as much as I need."

He smiled again and shrugged. "Your call."

I followed him back down to the front door. "Be sure to let me know today if you want it. I got two other people coming later."

I waved as I left. "You bet." I turned and hurried down the walkway to the sidewalk hoping to put as much space between Gerald and me as I possibly could as quickly as I could. I was starting to panic just slightly. Was this the only kind of place I could afford? I was so screwed.

As I sat on the bus on my way back downtown feeling sorry for myself, my phone pinged. It was Tom. "Finished at the house. They loved it. Back to you later."

Shit! I really did need to find somewhere to live. I hoped that the second place I was scheduled to see today had more to recommend it than this one.

I treated myself to lunch at a small café Joseph had recommended. It was bright and pretty with red and white gingham table cloths and white wrought-iron tables and chairs. The menu was full of French-inspired items like "*croque monsieur*" and "*crêpes.*" The prices were charmingly offered in Euros and dollars. I ordered crêpes and coffee and sat back as I tried to recover from my visit with Gerald. A shiver ran down my spine at the thought of having to live there. Maybe Tom could rent me a room. He probably had a big house with all that money he'd made from selling his internet business. He had said he wasn't married "yet" so there was probably a girlfriend. Maybe I could clean the house for them. I sighed. Being a starving artist wasn't all it was cracked up to be.

I finished lunch just in time to get to my next apartment. This one was a studio apartment in an old Victorian house on a tree-lined street. *This is more like it,* I thought as I turned into the walkway and up the three front steps onto the porch. I rang the bell.

Twenty seconds later, the door was opened by an older woman who smiled in recognition the minute I looked up from my phone.

"Charlotte Hudson!" she said. "Again, we reconnect."

It was Miss Davies. I could not have been more astonished.

"Come in, come in," she said. "My nephew didn't mention the name of the woman he said was coming by to see the studio." Then her face darkened. "I do have to be honest and tell you that I've shown it to another potential tenant already this morning. I hope you won't be disappointed." She gestured toward the porch. "I can access it through the house, but it does have its own outside door. Let's go in that way." She picked up a key ring from a table inside the door. I followed her back out onto the porch and down the steps.

There was another little walkway leading off the main one – one that I hadn't noticed before. It led to a side door three steps down. The door was painted a pretty robin's egg blue and was flanked by two urns out of which spilled all manner of beautiful greenery with bright red geraniums. I loved it at first glance. I could feel my excitement rising. It was lovely already.

Miss Davies unlocked the door and stepped aside to let me go in first. If this morning's monstrosity had smelled less than inviting, this one was a literal breath of fresh air. Everything about it was fresh. It looked as if it had just been painted, it was so bright and clean. It was a small studio with a darling kitchen kitted out with white cabinets and marble countertops (yes, marble). And there was a fireplace. There were two closets and a small bathroom with a stand-up shower that looked as if it had been newly renovated. I loved it. I could picture a writing desk under one of the two windows and plants keeping me company. I could see myself cooking in the tiny kitchen and even having someone over for dinner. I could picture a bed with a fluffy duvet and masses of pillows.

"I love it!" I blurted. "How much did you say it is a month?" It occurred to me that Miss Davies might be a bit lenient in the credit score and employment income checking thing that landlords did. It was perfect for me.

She gave me a number, and I think I gulped just a bit. I would certainly need to make myself available for more shifts at the library and sell a writing piece – or two. But I had to have it.

She smiled. "I'm so glad you like it, Charlotte. It's important to me to find a tenant whom I trust." She nodded at me encouragingly – a least it looked encouraging from where I was standing.

I followed her back out into the garden. She locked the door, and we walked back to the main walkway in front of the house. I could smell the roses blooming in a profusion of red and pink along the edges of the property. I could hardly believe my luck.

"Charlotte," she said hesitantly, "I must apologize for my abrupt departure the other day at the fabric store. Do forgive my rudeness."

"There's nothing at all to forgive."

She seemed relieved. "Well, then, I'll have my nephew call you tomorrow," Miss Davies said as we shook hands. "He looks after the letting of the studio for me."

"Looking forward to it!" I said as I waved.

I was feeling exceptionally optimistic a half an hour later when I unlocked the door of my mother's house, hoping that one of the three potential buyers might make an offer. I was ready. My phone pinged. It was Evelyn.

"How goes the house selling? Planning to come next week."

I sighed, but I knew it was inevitable. I only hoped that we'd have some kind of an offer to work with while she was here. Then I could think about decorating my new studio apartment. I could hardly wait to tell my writers' group about it. I wondered if I could fit them all in for a meeting? Maybe not, but I'd always thought it might make me feel more like a grown-up writer if I could host. Maybe someday.

That night I slept better than I had for months. Things were falling into place, and I'd soon be able to move on with my life.

~

I was just finishing my second cup of coffee the next morning while combing through more of the photos Mom had left behind when Tom called. "Do you have time to chat?" he said. I did.

It seemed that two of the parties of prospective buyers who had seen the house the day before were keenly interested.

"Wow, two! Are they interested enough to make an offer, or should I say offers?"

"Well," Tom said, "my clients seem very interested. They're working out a few details and said they'd get back to me later today. I'm not sure about the other agent's clients, although she did say to get ready for an offer this afternoon. They usually come through when they seem that definite but not always."

"So, we just wait?"

"Not exactly. I have two more prospects for tomorrow. You all right with prepping the house for another round of showings and making yourself scarce?"

I sighed. I was hoping that it might sell right out of the gate, but what choice did I have under the circumstances? "No problem."

Tom hung up, and I went back to the box of photos. I was scrutinizing each one lest I miss some clue to Mom's life pre-Dad, so the whole process was taking forever. If one of the prospective buyers did come through with an offer today or even in the next few days, I'd have to ramp up the work. I had no intention of taking boxes of unsorted photos to my new digs. But

I would be taking the sewing machine. That was a given at this point.

I had left the sewing machine set up under the window in my bedroom, and Lucinda had reluctantly allowed me to leave it there. At least I had removed it from the living room at her insistence. "I guess it could be deemed to be kitschy," she had finally conceded. Now I stood in the bedroom doorway and looked at it thoughtfully.

"Well, Junior, what stories could you tell me?" I asked it out loud. Was I now given to talking to inanimate objects? Oh well, it could be worse. I guess. I sat down on the stool in front of it. "Did Mom sit here in front of you when she made that dress in the photo? Are you older than I thought? Woodstock? Really?"

Junior remained silent.

I absently picked another photo. Mom (or her doppelganger – I hadn't come to any firm conclusion about this yet) was alone. She was wearing a sleeveless, gauzy sundress. She looked so happy in a faraway kind of way. Then I saw them. It was a stack of what appeared to be Bakelite bangles stacked up both arms. Every scrap of doubt that this was Mom vanished in an instant.

It was late that afternoon when the call came. It was Tom. "We have an offer." I could hear mounting excitement in his voice. "It's a good one. May I bring it over?"

I should not have hesitated for even a second but looked down at my sweat pants and the mess of ingredients that surrounded me on the counter where I had just started considering dinner. I'd have to clean up and change. Then I had an idea. "Sure. Why don't you stay so we can discuss it over dinner?"

The moment the words were out of my mouth, I regretted them. This would be so awkward – especially if he said no, he had to get home to have dinner with his girlfriend. I could feel my face beginning to redden. Although, does it really matter if there's no one there to see it?

"Sounds good," he said. Was that caution I heard in his voice? I was being ridiculous, and I knew it. "I'll bring wine. Or maybe champagne."

Was this a date or a client meeting to close a deal? Either way, I'd have to change my clothes.

Tom arrived an hour later bearing both a briefcase full of papers and two bottles – one of a Sancerre which I had never tasted as far as I knew and a bottle of champagne – *Veuve Clicquot* – which I'd tasted only once before in my life and swooned. I hoped we'd have a reason to crack that baby open.

Tom poured each of us a glass of Sancerre while I made sure the dinner wouldn't be ready for another hour or so while we looked at papers. We had decided that it might be better to go over the documents before we had imbibed much in the way of alcohol. I was tempted to ask Tom where his girlfriend was this evening but held my tongue out of an abundance of restraint.

"Sancerre is one of my favourite wines," he said as he passed me a glass. "I hope you like this one." I was sure I would. It was French, wasn't it?

We were going to have to sit in the kitchen to read the papers and to eat since the furniture in the dining room was owned by the staging company. It didn't look as if it could function in real life with its glass top and spindly legs – not to mention the "ghost" chairs as Lucinda had described the transparent plastic monstrosities that she had "paired" with it to use her designer lingo.

I took a sip of the wine and immediately wondered how much it had cost. It was divine. "Tom, this is fantastic. I hate to expose my ignorance of wines, but apart from it being French, I don't really know anything about it."

Tom sat down opposite me swirling his glass but not in that obnoxious, wine-snobby kind of way. "Yeah, I didn't know much, either until I sold my company. As a gift to myself, I went to Paris to take a two-week wine and spirit appreciation class at the *Cordon Bleu.*"

I was impressed. "So, did your girlfriend go with you?" Where in the world had that come from? Had I not learned to put my mind in gear before I put my mouth in motion? Again, the blurting was going to get me into embarrassing trouble.

Tom looked at me with an odd expression on his face. He pursed his lips slightly. "What? My girlfriend?"

I waved my hand dismissively. "Forget I even asked. What were you saying?" I inhaled a gulp of wine and began immediately coughing.

Tom got up to come around the table to pound me on the back. "Are you all right?"

I nodded through the tears that were streaming down my face, yet I was keenly aware that Tom had his hand on my back. I sort of hoped he'd leave it there.

He must have been convinced that I'd live. He removed his hand and took his place at the table across from me once again. "No, Charlie, my girlfriend didn't go with me."

Something clenched my heart. I was right. There was a girlfriend.

"She didn't go with me because I didn't invite her."

"You don't have to tell me anything. It's none of my business."

"Maybe not. But I want to tell you." He took a small sip of wine and gently placed the glass on the table.

"That was two years ago, and the reason I didn't invite her was that I wanted to put some distance between us. I figured that if we were apart for a couple of weeks, I'd be in a better headspace to..." He hesitated as if trying to find the best word. He shrugged. "To dump her."

I sipped my wine as daintily as I could to hide the smile that was forming on my lips against my attempts to stop it.

"I am girlfriend-less at this point in my life." He didn't look at me. "So, shall we review the offers?" A brilliant pivot, in my view.

There were two. I called Evelyn and put her on speaker so that the three of us could discuss strategy. As a litigator, Evelyn had talent in spades in that arena. The three of us agreed on a next step in the negotiation, then Evelyn clicked off. By the end of the evening, Tom and I had gotten to know one another better after some initial awkwardness, and I felt like I was developing a new friend. I hoped he felt the same. We were also coming very close to a deal on the sale of the house. I was elated.

Cleaning a kitchen had never been as blissful an experience as it was that evening after Tom left. I had reverted to my sweat pants and was humming along with the music I had playing on Mom's Bose system when the phone rang. It was Miss Davies's nephew. I thought I'd burst with happiness when I recognized the number.

"Ms. Hudson?" He sounded very professional. "I'm sorry to tell you that we've let the studio to another applicant."

And the bubble burst.

~

Evelyn's flight was scheduled to arrive at six p.m. The sale price for the house had finally been agreed upon, the papers had all been signed, and the young couple Tom had brought to see the house was expected to take possession at the end of September. Homelessness hovered over me like some kind of evil spectre. I had a couple of hours to myself after I finished my shift at the library, so I decided to take solace in a visit to *Sew Fine Things*. I figured I had time to make one more dress before I was going to be removed from my home. Joseph had offered to put me up for a month while I took the extra time to find a more permanent solution. It wasn't ideal (Joseph was so tidy and perfect), but it was amazing for him to offer. I'd have to find a place to store my meagre possessions, including the sewing machine, which I'd miss while in confinement with Joseph. I was feeling slightly unglued.

~

Al was behind the counter working on a laptop, which he quickly closed as I entered the store. He also closed two thick books that had been on the counter beside the laptop and slid them under the counter before I had a chance to see their titles. He smiled. "Charlie! Nice to see you. What pattern will you make this month?"

It had just occurred to me that I had, in fact, made a dress a month since the beginning of the year. I thought that it might be nice to make a few more, but that was now unlikely to happen, given my living arrangements.

"Charlie? What gives? You look sad."

I took three patterns out of my backpack. "Maybe a little, Al. This may be the last project I can take on for a while." I told him about the house selling and me losing the chance to live in my ideal little studio.

"You know the Dalai Lama?"

I was almost insulted. "Of course. Doesn't everyone?" I hoped that I didn't sound testy. If I did, he didn't let on.

"Okay, then, '*Remember that not getting what you want is sometimes a wonderful stroke of luck.*'"

Well, that one was familiar. That was the same quote I'd seen in the background of Grace, my YouTube sewing mentor's videos, so I nodded as if I agreed, but I was trying very hard not to let him see the tears that were beginning to form. I would not cry. "Sure. Luck." I pushed one of the patterns toward him. "What do you think of this one?"

It was a simple dress that was made of what was called colour blocking. Three different solid-colour fabrics were used to create interesting blocks and lines. When I had first picked the pattern out, I had a strange notion that it might make my life more interesting. Anyway, he nodded and left to retrieve three bolts of fabric. He laid them out on the counter in front of me. "What about these?"

I looked back and forth between the pattern and the fabrics. "I could use this one here and this one there." I pointed to the picture and the colour on the top half of the dress and the bottom right side of the skirt. I looked at it again and shook my head. "I'm not sure these will work, Al."

"Well, be flexible. Look at it from a different perspective." He moved the bolts so that the red one was at the top of the pile with a black and white one below.

I held the pattern next to the bolts now and smiled. "If something isn't working –"

"Try a new approach," Al said, smiling as he finished my thought.

~

When Evelyn arrived and dumped her suitcase on the kitchen floor on August 31, I was ready for her. She didn't have to search for wine or liquor today. I had it ready. I walked over to her and hugged her tightly, then stepped back and offered her the glass of wine. I wish I had taken a photo of the astonishment written all over her face. Then she smiled slightly and sat down.

"I think Michael is having an affair."

And my perfect sister with the perfect life collapsed like a house of cards.

September

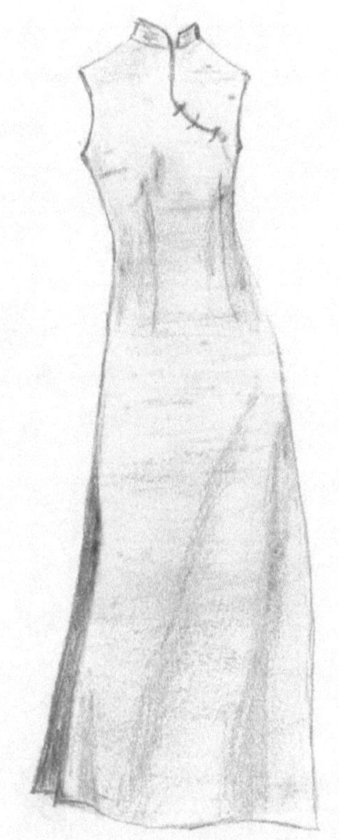

SEPTEMBER

The next morning was the first of September. The Labour Day weekend was upon us, a sure signal to the end of summer. When I awoke, I had such a hangover, I thought I might still be drunk. I couldn't remember ever having had that much to drink in my life. Evelyn and I had polished off two bottles of wine and most of a bottle of Jägermeister I had found months ago in the freezer. Why Mom had a bottle of Jägermeister in her freezer was past all comprehension. But then there seemed to be lots of things past all comprehension this morning.

If Evelyn and I had spent the evening before doing some kind of sisterly bonding over our respective calamitous situations, I couldn't remember. I only knew that we'd have to come clean about a few things, but before that could happen, I needed a shower – and a cup of coffee. Or two.

By the time I made my way down the hall and into the kitchen, Evelyn was already there. She had made coffee (thank goodness!) and seemed to be deeply involved in some kind of baking. But it couldn't be baking, could it? Evelyn never did anything remotely domestic. What in the world was going on? Apart from that little matter of her husband's alleged infidelity, of course.

She stood at the counter near the sink with her back to me. She gestured vaguely in the direction of the oven from which wonderful aromas were emanating. "The first batch is nearly done. Could you get the oven mitts and get them out when the timer goes off?"

I had no idea what was in the oven, but I was certainly in favour of assisting with whatever it was. The timer went off seconds later. I turned it off and proceeded to remove what turned out to be muffins from the oven then placed the pan on the trivet she had put on the counter beside the stovetop. When Evelyn turned around, she was holding another full muffin tin, which she placed in the still-hot oven.

"Evelyn, these look amazing! I didn't know you could bake muffins."

"There are lots of things you don't know about me, little sister."

Clearly, she was right.

"Would you like one with your coffee?" she said as she expertly removed them from the muffin tins. "They're lemon blueberry. I found some frozen blueberries. I hope you don't mind. I used them all."

I didn't mind at all. I used blueberries for yogurt smoothies, but this was so much better. We sat down with coffee and muffins and completely ignored the elephant in the room. Or perhaps elephants.

We sat, sipped and ate somewhat contentedly. Finally, I was starting to feel better. "How are you feeling this morning, Evelyn?"

"I'm great," she said without a hint of sarcasm. At least I couldn't discern any. "You?"

"Other than a headache, I'm fine." I chewed my second muffin more slowly than I'd inhaled the first one. "I think we should talk."

"Sure. About what?"

I wanted to slap her up the side of the head. I held myself back. "Well, let's start with Michael."

"What about Michael?" she said, completely avoiding looking at me.

"Evelyn, you can't just drop a bomb like 'I think Michael is having an affair' without further explanation."

"I can." She got up from the table and walked over to the sink. The window above the sink looked out into the over-grown garden in the back yard. I'd managed to keep the lawn in a reasonable condition all summer. I'd had several less than successful attempts to learn how to start the lawnmower – and let's not forget that it needed fuel periodically – before I could even manage that. But since I knew next to nothing about gardening, the other parts of the garden were beyond me. Evelyn stared out the window, her back to me. "It's hard for me," she said quietly.

"I know." I sat and waited for her to continue.

"Charlie, you cannot imagine what my life is like."

I had no doubt whatsoever that this was true. I could not imagine living in a fancy, professionally-decorated condo in a world-class city doing a job I loved that provided me with enough money to partake of the restaurants, the theatre, the symphony, the ballet, the cozy bars, the tony boutiques. Oh, and not to mention the good-looking, ambitious husband. She was certainly right about that. Was I jealous? Maybe. But I was not jealous of the great job or the handsome husband or even of the exciting city she lived in. But if I were being honest with myself, I had always been jealous of her sleek attractiveness, her deft ability to handle people and the way she had been able to succeed in accomplishing all her ambitions.

"Probably not," I said.

She was still staring out the window. "Michael doesn't want children."

"You don't either, so what's the issue?"

When she turned around, tears were running down her cheeks. "That's just it, Charlie. I do."

This was a stunning revelation to me. Even the day before she married Michael, she had told me one of the most important things about him was that he shared her ambition to be nothing more than a double-income-no-kids couple. They would work hard, travel far, do what they wanted. Forever. What had changed?

"Evelyn, you've never once even suggested that you wanted to have kids. Are you telling me that you've changed your mind? That motherhood is on your agenda now?"

She crumpled into the chair across from me. "Charlie, look around. Look at this house. I mean, if you look past the ridiculous staging. We grew up here. We had so many happy times. Do you remember those Saturday evening hamburger nights? Dad would fire up the barbeque – even in the winter – and we'd have hamburgers with cheese and mustard and relish. And we were allowed to have chips." She looked up at me. "Do you know how long it's been since I had potato chips?"

"Since the last time you and I got into them here?"

She nodded. "And that was the first time in forever."

I'd had chips two days earlier, but I hadn't eaten the whole bag (what do you take me for?). I wondered how many were left. I got up and opened the cupboard beside the refrigerator. Yes, the bag was there. "Do you still like chips with coffee?" I held the bag out.

Evelyn started laughing through her tears. "I do!"

I moved the bananas from the bowl on the counter and poured the rest of the chips into it. I didn't know how else to handle Evelyn right at that moment, but it occurred to me that this might just be a perfect way.

We sat in companionable silence for a few minutes sipping coffee and munching on sea salt potato chips. Then Evelyn began to talk, and I kept my mouth shut for a change. By the time she had finished, I realized that although I always thought I understood my perfect sister, I did not, and she was not perfect.

She was unhappy at her law firm – she'd been passed over for senior partner by what she described as an inferior male whose sycophantic ass-kissing skills rivalled those of Trump lackeys. She had begun to put out "feelers" as she put it to find another firm. She wanted to sell the condo and buy a house. Michael did not. She wanted to consider children in their future. Michael did not. She wanted to divorce Michael. Oddly, Michael did not want her to do that. So, she was here hiding out from him and trying to figure out what was going on in her life. Was Michael having an affair? Probably not. At least that's what he told her.

Then it was my turn. Where to begin?

"Evelyn, did Mom ever mention to you that she used to sew?"

"Sew? Sew what? Clothes?"

"Yeah. I found an old sewing machine in the basement hidden away under piles of boxes that were full of sewing patterns."

Evelyn thought for a moment. "Now that you mention it, I did see her looking at a sewing pattern one day when I was about nine or ten. At least I think it was a sewing pattern. I wasn't really paying attention to tell you the truth. Where's the sewing machine now? Is it the one you used to make that hideous shower curtain monstrosity of a so-called dress?"

And…she was back. The Evelyn I knew and loved. It made me kind of happy.

"I have something to show you." I got up and gestured for her to follow me. I walked down the hall and into my bedroom, where the sewing machine was sitting under the window. I had also recently acquired one of those rolling clothes racks, which I had placed along the wall next to the window. On the rack were the dresses I had created. There were now eight of them.

Evelyn walked over to the sewing machine and ran her hand over the top of it. Then she looked at the rack of dresses. "I don't understand."

So, I told her the story. I told her about finding the machine and the patterns. I told her about my foray into sewing. While I was telling her about Al and his shop, she was rummaging through the dresses as if she were in a boutique searching for something to wear to an event. She looked at each one in turn. When I had finished describing the boxes of patterns, she sat on the side of the bed and looked at me.

"Is that it? Have you been sewing dresses for the past eight months?"

I wasn't sure where she was going with this. Was she accusing me of shirking my duties? Was she suggesting that the house would have been prepped earlier if I had focused on it?

"Well, I haven't actually spent eight months doing it. I did one a month." I smiled as I said this. I really had made a dress a month, as I realized the last time I visited Al. "It was kind of like therapy, you know."

"I wish," she said quietly, almost wistfully. "So, why didn't you tell me about this?"

"I'm not sure, sis. I guess I thought you'd find it weird or a waste of time."

"I probably would have," she said. "But now? I'm not so sure. Where are those patterns?"

I hauled the boxes out of the closet, and we sat on the floor and began exploring them. Evelyn seemed oddly delighted as she pulled them out in handfuls. "Look at this!" she said, then, "Wow! I love this one!" I had no idea that she was as fascinated by vintage designs as I was.

Then she sat back. “Why do you suppose Mom never told us about this?” she said as she examined another pattern envelope. “And why didn’t she ever make any clothes for us?” I could hear genuine disappointment in Evelyn’s voice.

I had wondered the same thing. It was nice to be able to discuss this with someone who understood my bafflement.

“There’s something else,” I said, getting up from the floor and going to the closet to retrieve another box. “These photos.” I started opening the box and removing the photos I’d already sorted through.

Evelyn came over and started looking at them. “Who are all these people?”

I shrugged. “No idea.” I hesitated for a moment then pulled the picture with the one recognizable face out of the folder. I had put it there so it wouldn’t get mixed up with the others. I handed it to her. “Here.”

As she looked at the grainy photograph, I tried to discern if there was any recognition in her reaction. “Okay, who’s this?” She didn’t seem to have seen the familiar face. She turned it over. “Woodstock?”

“Take a closer look at the woman in the picture.”

She did. “What the actual f**k? It’s Mom?”

“Looks that way,” I said.

"Who the f**k is looking at her as if he's madly in love with her?" Evelyn may not have been the most romantic person I knew, but she seemed to be able to discern the look of love!

"That's just it. I have no idea. I thought you might know."

She shook her head. "Are there any more photos of Mom from back then?" She started rifling through the layers of photos.

"There's this one." I handed her another photo.

"Oh my actual god, Charlie," she said, staring at the photo in her hand. "Look at the bracelets. She had them long before she married Dad."

Two hours later, we had all the photos laid out on the floor in the living room. I had sort of organized them already, but with Evelyn's help, I was able to identify even more of the photos by era. There were hundreds of pictures from long before even Mom and Dad had been born then photos of the two of us in our early years when people still sent photos off to be printed. We had to guess at the decades in many cases. By the time we got to the end of all of them, we had only six photos from the same era as the Woodstock one – at least that's what it looked like to us. We put all of them away except for those six.

We passed them back and forth, taking our time to examine each one in turn. There was that one of Mom with the unidentified guy at Woodstock and the one of her alone wearing all the bracelets. Then there was one of Mom with two other young women wearing similar versions of the hippie dress she was wearing. It seems that even hippies had uniforms. That one seemed to have been taken at Woodstock as well. We didn't recognize either of the other two girls. A fourth photo was a group shot – also clearly at Woodstock.

There were about ten young people in it. The sun was shining, and they all seemed to be happily leaning on one another. The young man in the centre of the picture was bare-chested and had his arms raised as he flashed peace signs to whoever was taking the picture. It was the same young man as in the photo with Mom.

The fifth photo was another one of Mom by herself. She was sitting on the ground amid a morass of humanity. She was hugging her knees into herself with a dreamy expression on her face.

The last one was of a young soldier. We both peered closely at it and recognized that it was the same young man as in the photo with Mom. It was a close-up headshot. He was looking up into the camera, a half-smile on his face. The helmet he was wearing had a ribbon around it that said: "War is hell." Vietnam. There was no doubt about it. We turned it over. The unfamiliar handwriting on the back said, "Love you forever, Chuck."

"Who the hell is Chuck, and why did Mom have his photo hidden away?"

I wasn't listening. I was staring at the group photo. Something clicked. "Evelyn," I said, pointing at the young woman next to Mom. "Isn't that Miss Davies?"

"What? The old bat who used to teach that stupid Family and...what was it?"

"Consumer Studies."

She grabbed the picture from me and started looking at all the faces. "I don't know. I didn't know her as well as you did. I mean, I had her for a semester, but I never paid much attention to her classes. Sewing wasn't really my thing. I suppose it could be her. But then again...Anyway, why in the world would she be in Woodstock with Mom? For that matter, what the actual f**k was Mom doing there anyway? It was so not her scene."

It seemed to me that it wasn't Miss Davies's scene either, but there they were. In Woodstock. In 1969. Together. And who was Chuck?

~

Life has a funny way of throwing us curves. There's an old saying Mom used to paraphrase and quote to us mostly throughout our angst-ridden teenage years:

Want to make god laugh? Tell her your plans. God must really be laughing at me now. I'd made plans – sort of. But none of them had materialized in the way I had lived them in my mind. Now that the house had been sold, I had to find a place to live or being roomies with Joseph was going to become a reality.

Evelyn offered to help me look. I don't think she was quite able to get her head around the fact that I didn't have the kind of money she did – even with my share of the house proceeds. Over the next few days, we looked at three places together and at the end of the last one, I told her that she couldn't come anymore.

"Why not? I know a lot about apartments."

"These aren't the kind of apartments you know something about," I said, exasperated at her reactions to the showings. She had sighed and kvetched at every one of them. Too small. Too noisy. Too grimy. Not in a good part of town, and on and on. I'd had it.

"Well, you have to live somewhere, and I can't have my sister living in a dump."

"Why not? I've probably been living in a dump from your perspective for years now. You never saw the flat I shared for the past few years." We were having dinner. Evelyn had made spaghetti and meatballs, which was surprisingly good. She truly was full of surprises. I expertly twirled my spaghetti with spoon and fork, I skill I had assiduously cultivated for some years. "I suppose you feel guilty."

She almost choked. "Guilty?" She drew her paper napkin across her mouth. "Why in the world would I feel guilty?"

"I don't know," I said. "Maybe because I stayed and you left, and now you have a beautiful condo and a terrific wardrobe, and I have –"

"Dresses you've made while following your writing bliss," she finished.

She had a point. Just then, her phone rang. When she picked it up and looked at the caller ID, her face drained of all colour. "It's Michael. I'm going to have to talk to him." She got up and fled to her room, noisily closing the door behind her.

I got up and started cleaning up the kitchen. I was just finishing putting everything in the dishwasher when my phone rang. It was Tom.

"Hey, Charlie," he said. "Have a moment to talk?"

"What's up? No problem with the sale?"

"No, nothing like that. Everything is all set to close at the end of the month."

"Great," I said. "Lucinda's stagers are coming tomorrow to remove all their stuff, and I'll be getting rid of the other extraneous furniture that's still in the basement."

"The buyers have a request. It turns out they can't move in until Christmas, and they're planning a few renovations before then. They're wondering if you know anyone who might be interested in house-sitting for a few months."

"Uh, yes, I believe I do." I could feel the smile overtaking my face.

And just like that, I didn't need to look at any more apartments. At least not for a few more months. *Wow*, I was thinking, *is this how prisoners on death row feel when they get that reprieve?* Well, that might have been a bit over-dramatic, but it was a weight lifted off me nevertheless. In any case, I think, in that moment, I understood the Dalai Lama by way of Grace and Al. Perhaps not getting that studio with Miss Davies might just have been my stroke of luck after all. And the truth is that I am well aware that luck can be short-lived, but I'll take it.

~

Evelyn and I stood on the front porch, both us of us with our arms folded across our chests the next morning as we watched Lucinda's stagers close the truck. They had just removed the couches, chairs, rugs, toss cushions and sculptural whatnots from the living room, dining room, hall and Mom's bedroom. We had been living with old furniture in both our original bedrooms.

"So, you're going to live in an empty house just to avoid having to make a decision about where to live?" Evelyn at her finest.

"What I'm going to do is move the sewing machine into the living room and work there right in front of the picture window."

Evelyn made a face as she turned to go back into the house. When I finally followed her, I found her standing in the middle of the empty living room.

"Speaking about decisions," she said, "whatever happened to that private high school that offered you a chance to teach writing last year?"

"I turned them down," I said.

"Geezus, Charlie, don't you think it's time you got a real job? Opportunities like that don't come along all the time. You can't spend your whole life chasing a dream. It's a bit quixotic, don't you think?"

"Maybe I *am* tilting at windmills as they say, but you don't know what it's like to have this kind of dream."

She turned around and looked at me straight in the face, her arms crossed even more tightly across her chest. "Who do you think you are? Do you think you're the only person in the world who ever wanted to pursue a passion and make a career out of it?"

I knew I wasn't, but I didn't know where she was going with this, so I simply shrugged.

"I wanted to be an actor, you know."

This was quite a stunning revelation to me. Had I missed the signs of a budding artist? "I remember you doing all those plays in junior and senior high school," I said, "but it never occurred to me that you wanted to actually *be* an actor." I was trying to remember if I had ever once gotten the impression that she wanted to pursue acting in any real way. I got nothing. "Did you?"

"Well, thanks for asking. Finally. And yes, I had a secret dream to be an actor. But I also have a very practical side to my nature as I'm sure you know only too well. So, I decided I'd take my acting chops and passion to another stage."

"You became a litigator." Now I got it. "But you didn't try to be a professional actor."

"You make it sound as if I settled for second best. I don't see it that way. I see it as taking stock of my talents and finding a place where I could use them while at the same time making a living. The whole question of how to pay the bills is immediately gone from the equation, and I can concentrate on being the best actor I can be – to the benefit of my clients, not just myself."

"Are you suggesting that I'm only focused on myself?"

"The question answers itself."

I would have been angry beyond all proportions if it had not been so patently clear that she was right. I took a deep breath before I spoke. "Easy for you to say when you have a variety of natural gifts to choose from."

It was her turn to get angry. "Charlotte Hudson, you are sometimes the densest person I know. You have as many, if not more, natural gifts as I do, but you choose to ignore them. Do you think I encouraged you to take that teaching job so just so I could see you with a real job?"

"Well, it certainly looked that way to me."

"You are beyond maddening sometimes. I know that you're a talented writer." I started to speak, but she held up her hand. "I've read every single magazine piece you've ever written. And what's more, I read your writing journals when you were in high school." She held up her hand again. "I realize that sounds like I was snooping, but I loved your stories. I always knew you had talent. I was actually a tiny bit jealous. But you were also wonderful with those kids you used to work with in the after-school program." She sat down on the floor as if she had suddenly been hit by a wave of weariness.

Back in high school, I had spent many happy hours after school with kids in grades six and seven. We created characters and stories together. I loved it, and I guess they did too. I remembered one of the kids telling me that she wanted to be just like me when she grew up – a writer and storyteller. I smiled at the memory.

"Charlie, you're a natural-born teacher. You're a natural-born storyteller and writer. And you have a Master's degree in Fine Arts. Why in the world would you pass up that opportunity?"

In that moment, I realized that I didn't have an answer.

"You don't have to choose between the two, Charlie. You never did."

~

I needed a fabric fix. More to the point, I think I needed to chat with Al. He always seemed to have a *bon mot* for me just when I needed one. But when I arrived at *Sew Fine Things*, he wasn't there. The woman I'd seen in the shop on two earlier occasions greeted me.

"Good afternoon," she said as I closed the door behind me. I could see that there was one other customer in the store – a young man who was far down the aisle in front of me, examining bolts of fabric. "How may I help you?" Then she looked at me closely. "Are you by any chance Charlie?"

"I am." I smiled at her.

"I suppose you are looking for Alvaro."

I was puzzled for just a moment, then I remembered. The last time I'd encountered her in the shop, she'd mentioned that Alvaro was Al's real name. "Yes. Is he here today?" I was certainly hoping he was.

She shook her head. "He is away but mentioned that should you appear in the store, I am to assist you. He has told me about you and your new interest in sewing."

Without Al, it seemed that I was being left to my own devices today to choose a pattern. The truth is that I could always do this in any case, but my little ritual, whereby Al made the final choice, was something I realized I had grown to cherish. I plunged my hand into my backpack and took out the first pattern I put my hand on. I think I gasped a little. It was a pattern for a dress I had long coveted. Although the pattern was from the 1960s, it was a dress that would look modern in any century. It was for an Asian-inspired dress with a high, Mandarin-style collar and placket that extended from the centre of the front to the armhole. The placket was held closed by those frog things. I placed it on the counter.

"This is wonderful," she said, picking it up. "A cheongsam. How very lovely."

I had not known until that moment that the proper term for these Asian dresses was cheongsam. I'd have to write that down.

Then she looked me up and down. "You will have to alter the pattern," she said. "But it will look wonderful on you. Do you plan to make the long one?" Before I could answer, she said, "Of course you do!"

I loved the full-length version, but I couldn't think of a single place I could wear it. "It's not that practical," I said finally.

"Practical is over-rated. Come with me." She led me to the back of the store, and through a small door that led to another room I had never been in before.

The room was a dazzling display of colours. The shelves were very neatly arranged and contained bolts of what looked to me like brocade with its detailed designs that resemble embroidery. There was also an astounding number of bolts of what looked like silk shantung, that beautifully textured, rich-looking silk that I'd seen on high-end fashion runways. And the colours! Fabulous jewel tones of red, turquoise, emerald green – they were fantastic to the eye. This must be where they kept the really good stuff. There was a small counter in the middle of the room. The woman, whose name I still didn't know (she hadn't offered it), removed four bolts from the shelving and placed them on the table. One was black with a red design, the second white with a pale blue design, the third was red with a very fine black design. The fourth bolt was pure red shantung. "Please," she said, gesturing for me to come closer. "You must touch the brocade and the shantung. They are pure silk."

I was almost afraid to touch them, but I think I might have been even more afraid of the price tag. "I don't think I have the skills to work with this yet," I said as I stroked the piece of red shantung. I could not take my eyes off it.

"You must stick with it. How do you say it in English?" she said although I thought that her English was perfectly fine. "Tenacious. Yes, you must be tenacious." She moved the other bolts away. "I see that this one has spoken to you, so you must have it."

She began to roll the fabric off the bolt while I held my breath as she proceeded to cut the piece. I squeezed my eyes shut for a moment and contemplated how I would feel when I had to actually cut into it myself. I was still reeling a half an hour later. It had indeed been eye-wateringly expensive – at least in my current circumstances – but I figured it was my gift to myself from the proceeds of the house sale that would be in my bank account in another week. With that justification settled, I decided to take a walk.

Two blocks later, I found myself standing in a bookstore flipping through books. I loved bookstores but increasingly read only in electronic format. It was kind of a shame since I truly love the feel of a real book in my hands. Maybe that's why I loved working at the library. I walked up and down a few aisles in this small space, stopping in front of a table of books by the late Stephen Hawking. He seemed to be a favourite of one of the bookstore employees. I picked one up randomly and began flipping through the pages enjoying the feel of real paper under my fingers. When I stopped flipping, I looked up at the poster above the table.

It read: "*Remember to look up at the stars and not down at your feet. However difficult life may seem, there is always something you can do and succeed at. It matters that you don't just give up.* ~ Stephen Hawking."

October

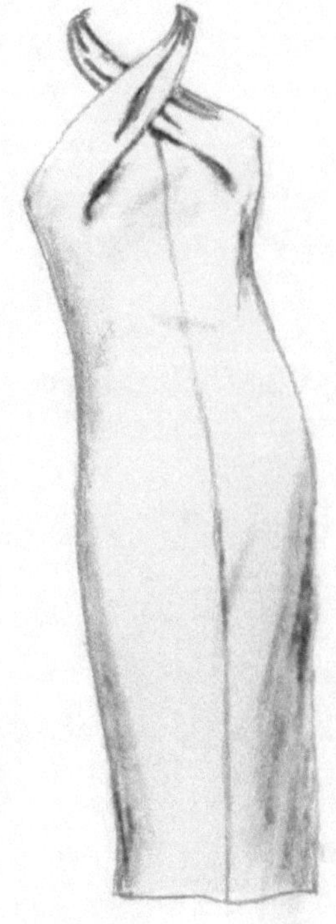

The final sale of the house went without a hitch. I had been holding my breath as Evelyn and I walked into our lawyer's office on the closing day to sign the papers and leave the keys. I had kept one set for myself since I was to be the temporary tenant. Then we went out to brunch and waited for the final word from Tom that everything was finalized. While I was savouring the last bite of my Eggs Benedict, Tom called tell us that the buyers' final "walk-through" had gone flawlessly. The cheques were being deposited into our bank accounts as we spoke. I had breathed out and ordered another round of mimosas. While we were enjoying our bubbles and orange juice, Evelyn told me about what she had found when I left her alone in the house while I visited *Sew Fine Things*.

She had been rummaging through the boxes in my closet and had found the unfinished "wedding dress." She had been as perplexed as I was about whose it was, why it was unfinished and why our mother had been keeping it. I had no more answers now than I had when I had first discovered it. We decided that it might remain one of those unsolved mysteries of life.

"I guess we should just get rid of it, then," she said.

I demurred. I didn't bother telling her that I had no intention of throwing it out. I doubted that she'd care much since her own life was about to get a whole lot more complicated if she went ahead with her plans to give Michael the ultimatum she'd decided on. Children or a divorce. I didn't envy her one bit anymore. When we finished and paid the bill, Evelyn called a taxi (there was still no Uber here, a situation that she lamented every time she visited) and left for the airport.

~

As it turned out, the renovations the new owners planned to do weren't nearly as invasive as I had feared. I thought my life for the next couple of months might consist of marshalling workers and looking for an apartment. But it wasn't so bad.

A week after the sale had been completed, a brightly painted pick-up truck arrived, and two young men and a young woman jumped out at seven a.m. I was grateful they didn't need access to the interior of the house at that hour. I had received a text from the new owners the day before telling me that the landscapers would be arriving. They wanted to manicure the place before the winter set in. I couldn't blame them for that.

An hour after they arrived, I peeked out the window while sipping my coffee to find them hard at work, pruning trees and removing dead wood from the bushes that lined the edges of the backyard, up against the fence. Given that they appeared to be twentysomethings, I expected to find at least two of them scrolling through a smartphone. I was so wrong, and for the first time in my life, I realized that I was now the "older" person making judgements about the "younger" people. It wasn't pretty. What was happening to me?

By mid-morning, I figured it was coffee time. I got up from my desk, where I'd been wrestling with a magazine piece that was due in a week and went outside into the October sunshine to see if they might enjoy a cup of coffee. I also had some cookies I'd bought at a cookie shop I'd discovered three doors down from the fabric store. I really needed to share them, or at the rate I was going through them, I'd need more than a new apartment – I'd need a diet doctor as well.

The three of them introduced themselves as Jake, Kyle and Jess.

"Hey, thanks," Jake said as I offered him a cookie. He took a chocolate one. "Cool place."

"Yeah," I said, "I lived here as a kid. Now I'm house-sitting."

"Awesome," Jess said as she looked around the yard. "It must be kind of weird to be here, though." She ran her fingers through the long blonde ponytail poking out from the hole in the back of her baseball cap that sported the brightly-coloured company logo.

"So, are you three spending a semester off school?" I had no real idea how old they were. They looked to me as if they might be somewhere between their last year in high school and their first year in university.

The three of them laughed at that. "Not exactly," Jake said. "This is our business. School wasn't, like, doing it for us. You know how it is." I didn't really.

"I was a chem major. It was, like, not at all what I thought it would be," Kyle said. "I was good at it in high school, but it wasn't my jam. You know?"

Jake chimed in that he had been a biology major headed for medical school. Jess had been studying political science with a view to law school. All had evidently had a kind of come-to-Jesus moment at about the same time. They all discovered that higher education might not be for them.

"This is great, then," I said seriously impressed by the fact that these three (very) young people had that kind of entrepreneurial spirit. "Your parents must be proud of what you're accomplishing." God, I sounded like an elder. But I suppose I was. I had at least ten years on them, which made me an old millennial and them something like generation Z, maybe?

"Kidding, right?" Jake said. "I thought my dad was going to have a coronary on the spot. He was way past angry."

"Yeah," Jess said. "Jake's dad is a big-time surgeon. He doesn't get it, but the truth is that we're happier than we've ever been and will probably be able to hire some university students next summer. I've even got my own apartment. I don't even have to share!" She beamed.

I was somewhat in awe of them. And as the day wore on, I realized that they not only loved what they were doing, but they were also good at it. When they had finished, the yard looked immaculate and, dare I say it, loved. Interesting.

The next group of workers arrived two days later, bringing along a variety of oddly-shaped pieces of wood and plastic things I didn't recognize. Two older men were in the back yard for three hours putting together what turned out to be an exceptionally elaborate jungle gym with turrets, slides and, of course, swings. I almost wished that I was five years old again. It looked like serious fun. I snapped a picture of it and texted it to Evelyn.

"I want one," she texted back.

Tom called later that day. I thought I might never hear from him again now that the house sale was completed.

"Let's go to dinner," he said.

I said yes.

"Let's dress up," he said. "I have a place I'd love to have you come with me, but it's a bit upscale."

Upscale sounded good to me. "So, I'm thinking smart casual?"

"Think upmarket glamorous. Cocktail?"

What in the world would I wear?

I had four days to consider this situation. I wasn't at all certain I had anything that could remotely be considered to be "upmarket glamorous" or even vaguely "cocktail" in my wardrobe. My wardrobe ran to the less-than-smart-casual kind. I had jeans galore and a few nice sweaters. I also owned a suit for some unknown reason. I couldn't remember what I'd been thinking when I made that purchase. So, of course, I went to my rolling rack next to my sewing machine and started to make my way through the dresses as Evelyn had done. I was 'shopping my closet' as they say these days.

Of course, the first few weren't suitable for public consumption – I saw that now. Evelyn – and Miriam and Joseph – were right. That first one was indeed hideous. I was actually kind of embarrassed now when I thought about it. But the most recent one...the red silk cheongsam... It had been a struggle, but I'd finished it. And it was beautiful even if I did say so myself. I lifted it off the rack and held it up against myself. I looked down and tried to picture myself somewhere upmarket glamorous or having cocktails, and I could almost feel it in this dress. I took it into my bedroom, where the full-length mirror remained and scrutinized it. If I didn't take advantage of this opportunity to wear it, another might not arise for a very long time. And remember those cookies? If I kept eating them, it might never fit again, anyway. It was glamorous, there was no doubt about that, but I had opted for the full-length version. It now occurred to me that it might be a bit much. I was surprisingly disappointed. I put it back on the rail and sat down at the sewing machine. What now?

I had two choices. I could go to a boutique of some kind and get help from one of those annoying little shop girls. You know the ones. They are otherwise known as today's self-appointed arbiters of style. I would then come home with some version of what one of them thinks an "older" woman ought to wear to cocktails, or I could go to *Sew Fine Things*, buy some fabric and spend the next four days madly sewing. No contest. I was in the fabric shop three hours later with a single vintage sewing pattern clutched to my chest.

~

I felt a giddy sense of relief as I walked through the door of the shop, and the little bell jangled to herald my arrival. There was Al, standing on a small ladder, rearranging bolts of fabric on the shelves next to the counter. He turned and smiled broadly.

"Hello, Al," I said as I swung my backpack off my shoulders and laid it on an empty spot on the counter next to the cash register.

"Hello yourself, Charlie," he said as he made his way down the three steps. "Sorry I missed you last time."

"So, you know I made a dress in September?"

"Of course," he said. "And I know you chose a red silk. Photos? I need to see photos!"

I had a few selfies stored on my phone. I knew they weren't the best pictures, but the one I took into the full-length mirror caught it all.

He whistled softly as he scrolled through them. "Charlie, do you realize how far you've come?"

He had no idea.

He rubbed his hands together. "What do you have in this month's plans?"

"I need a cocktail dress. I mean, I need something for some kind of upscale, glamorous thing I've been invited to. I'm not really sure about details, but that much I know. And I need it within four days." I placed the pattern I'd been carrying onto the counter. "I think this is the one."

Al picked it up, looked at it briefly and shook his head. "Upscale glamorous?" He tapped the pattern drawings with his finger. "This won't cut it, Charlie, and I'm betting you know that."

"Maybe," I said, pouting like some kind of petulant child, "but I don't have much time."

It was a simple, sleeveless sheath, something that I could probably make in my sleep at this stage. It was safe, and I needed safe. At least I thought I did.

"I could sell you something that would make this simple pattern work for something glamorous, but I think you'd be selling yourself short." He looked down at the pattern again then at me. "I'm guessing that you've been invited to this soirée by someone special."

I think I actually blushed. He was enough of a gentleman to not mention it. "It's just dinner."

"Is it?" He looked down at the pattern again. "This is too safe. What else are you hiding in that backpack?"

I did have two other options in my bag. I had considered not bringing them along, but something had propelled me to stuff them in anyway. I took them out now and put them on the counter beside the other one.

"No contest," he said, moving the original one and one of the other ones to the side, thus leaving a single pattern in the middle of the counter. "This is the one."

I took in a deep breath. It was a pattern for a dress that I absolutely loved but felt strongly that I wouldn't be able to pull off. It wasn't that I didn't think I could sew it – although whether I could do a good enough job for this kind of occasion was still an open question in my mind – it was more that I wasn't at all sure I could wear it. After all, I'd spent months making tents to hide under. But this one...

It was another sheath, but in this design, the fabric came up over the bust, crossed in front just at the nape of the neck and then went around the neck fastening as a halter behind the neck. The back was cut low, and the shoulders were alluringly bare. It was so not me, I thought. But I loved it. I could see Evelyn wearing it but would never have considered it for myself in my previous life.

"I don't know who else will be at this event I've been invited to, but I'm fairly sure that I can't hold a candle to them. This person who invited me has a lot of money."

Al shook his head. "Charlie, you and I are going to find the most fantastic fabric for this dress – I'm thinking cream-coloured silk crepe, lined with silk charmeuse."

I think I winced. As you already know, I'd taken to running my hands over bolts whenever I was in the shop dreaming of the day when I might actually wear something as soft and delicious as silk charmeuse. But what I was thinking at that moment was that I had read it was notoriously difficult to sew – as slippery and thin as it is.

He brought out the bolts of fabric, and I almost swooned as I ran my hand over them, feeling their soft lusciousness. "I don't know, Al. Could I really pull this off?"

"If you mean the sewing, yes. The other? Eleanor Roosevelt once said, '*Remember, no one can make you feel inferior without your consent.*'" He expertly wielded his shears, cut the lengths of fabric and folded them. "Withhold consent, Charlie."

~

The next morning, I laid out the silk crepe on the floor of the living room. As I did, I began to panic. I was in over my head. How would I ever do this in three days and be sure that it would be suitable for public consumption? I stood above the beautiful fabric and remembered what Al had said to me months ago – and a lesson that I didn't seem to have learned yet. He had quoted Plato to me: "*The first and best victory is to conquer self.*" Perhaps it was time I took that to heart. So, with shaking hands, I began cutting this beautiful fabric. Self-confidence or not, though, it wasn't long before I realized something else: over-confidence might be just as problematic. At some point, I just knew I'd need a bit of help if I wanted to be sure this was ready by Friday night.

Although I was still annoyed with Miss Davies because of the studio (in her defence, she had emailed me an apology – evidently, her nephew had also shown it the same day and had promised it to his friends). I wondered if I might be able to consult her and garner a bit of mentorly support.

I called her that evening. She seemed more than delighted to be able to help. She said she' be over in the morning.

So, at nine a.m. the next morning, Miss Davies arrived carrying a large black tote over her shoulder. In that tote were her sewing supplies: scissors and shears, needles, threads of all sorts including silk and cotton, marking chalks, and so much more. She was ready. I was getting there.

By the time we were finished for the day, the dress was fitted to me beautifully. I had also completed some of the detailing of the bodice with a little help from my new friend. There was more work to do, but I now felt as if I could handle it myself. I guess I had learned to be tenacious.

"It's going to be beautiful on you, Charlotte," Miss Davies said as she tidied up her materials and stowed them back in the tote. "Who's the lucky man?"

I think I blushed. "How did you guess?"

"You have a reason for wanting this dress to be perfect, and it shows. I hope he appreciates it, whoever he is."

"So do I." It suddenly struck me that now was the perfect moment to pounce on her. Well, maybe I'd avoid pouncing; instead, I would sidle into it. "Miss Davies," I said, choosing my words carefully. "you mentioned you knew my mother when she was my age. How well did you know her?"

Her back was to me, but I noticed an almost imperceptible change in her shoulders. A slight movement that signified – I didn't know what. Then she turned around. There was something different in her eyes. It struck me that they looked younger. I wasn't sure what made it seem that way to me, but it did.

"We were good, perhaps even best friends for a time, Charlotte. I suppose I knew her quite well."

"I found a photo."

"Just one?" She smiled a kind of half-smile.

The photo box was now in the living room. I'd bought a faux leather-covered box at one of those off-price home-decorating shops so I could keep the special photos – photos of people Evelyn and I actually recognized – separate from the others we planned to get rid of. I went over and took the smaller box out. I opened it and removed the photo that was second from the top. I handed it to her.

Miss Davies's hand flew to her mouth, and tears started forming at the corners of her eyes. "Oh, Charlotte," she said, "I haven't seen this picture in years." She looked at it thoughtfully. "We were so young."

"What were you and Mom doing at Woodstock?"

"I suppose we were doing what everyone was doing. Listening to music, smoking dope and..." she stopped and looked at me. "Your mother never told you about this, did she?"

I shook my head. "And what else were you doing?"

"I was going to say 'making love,' but that sounds a bit too grand."

I thought I might swallow my tongue. I was so dumfounded to hear anyone refer to my mother in those terms. Psychedelic rock music? The dope? The making love? Whatever that meant back in 1969 at Woodstock in the middle of a massive crowd of grimy hippies. At least that's how it looked to me. God, I *was* judgmental – and even about my own mother.

"Tell me about it. Please?"

"It's true that your mother and I were good friends back in those days."

"But you and Mom weren't friends as far as I knew. She never once mentioned she knew you. Did you two have a falling out?"

"In a manner of speaking," she said, taking a deep breath. She looked at the photo again. "There must have been reasons why your mother didn't tell you about her life before she met your father. I'm not sure I have the right to do it."

"Mom's dead. I don't think she cares now." I took the photo from her. "Who's this guy?" I pointed to the love-struck guy, then pulled the other photo of him in the army helmet out of the box and passed it to her.

She stared silently at the picture for a moment then touched it as if she were touching his face. "This was taken in Vietnam," she said quietly as if trying to keep any emotion she felt from bubbling up to the surface. She turned the photo over and seemed startled by the writing on the back. "This must have been just before he was killed." Tears now ran down her cheeks. She looked up at me. "Charlotte, I promise I will tell you about him, but not today. Come for coffee on Sunday, and we'll talk."

With that, she picked up her tote bag and left. I looked down at the photos in my hands and realized I was crying, too. But I didn't know why.

~

On Thursday morning, Miriam called me. "Charlie dear, I am demolished, but we must cancel this evening's meeting."

I couldn't in my wildest imaginings be "demolished" by having to skip a meeting, but I didn't share that with Miriam. "Is everything okay?"

"It is not," she said. I thought I could hear her sipping on something – I hoped it was coffee at this hour and not gin. That would suggest things were bad, indeed. It hadn't happened for a long time, but Miriam had been prone to drinking whenever she faced a personal setback. "Wendy's children have some kind of intestinal distress, and Karl has been called out on the road to cover for an emergency." She sipped again. "So, we would be only three, and I'm feeling a bit under the weather myself."

I was sorry to hear that but wondered if being "under the weather" might be accounted for by drinking so early. I had concluded that she was, in fact, not drinking coffee. Anyway, I had been looking forward to showing them photos of my newest creations, but it wasn't to be. And after all, the meeting was for sharing writing, not sewing. This would give me a bit more time for the finishing touches on the dress anyway. And there was the matter of Miss Davies and the photos. I had a lot to think about.

~

When Tom arrived at my door on Friday evening, I was ready. I had even bought a new pair of shoes and had found a beaded clutch bag in Mom's closet when I'd been clearing it out a few months earlier. I had saved it because I had seen it in a photo of Mom and Dad on their way to some kind of event. It was a bit of nostalgia. My only problem was what to wear over the dress. October evenings aren't exactly warm in this part of the world. I rummaged through Evelyn's room in the hope that, in her state of uncertainty, she might have left something behind on her last trip. I was in luck.

Hanging on a hanger in the far corner of her closet was a lone scarf. It was one of those pashmina things, but I figured it was probably the real thing – silk and cashmere – not one of those rayon ones. I checked the label. I was right. Real pashmina it was. The only problem with it was that it was red. But I thought that it would have to do. At least it didn't clash with ivory!

When I opened the door, Tom was standing on the front porch clutching a bouquet of red roses and a bottle of champagne. But that's not what caught my eye. He was also attired in what is probably referred to as "creative black-tie." He was wearing a tuxedo jacket, formal white shirt and red bow tie. The tuxedo pants were skinny, and he was wearing black loafers without socks. I was stunned – in a good way. But he seemed just as stunned.

"Charlie, you look incredible."

I did a little twirl. "Thanks!" I was unbelievably happy that he seemed to notice. But then again, he had always liked me anyway!

We had time to open the champagne and have a glass or two each before we were ready to go. He called a taxi for us. When I threw the red pashmina around me, we both laughed. We looked as if we had planned the matching scarf and bow tie. Off we went arm-in-arm.

On the ride to the event, Tom explained to me that he may not have been quite as forthcoming about dinner as he might have been. It turned out we were headed to dinner, of course, but it was part of a fund-raiser for a literacy charity he supported in a big way.

"I was afraid that if I told you, you might not want to come with me, and I really wanted you to. I'd like to have you with me." Frankly, I couldn't have cared less as long as we were going to be doing it together. It was, after all, a date.

It was being held at a private club that I, of course, had never been inside. I should have been more nervous than I was. Maybe it was the champagne. Or maybe I'd taken heed of Al's Eleanor Roosevelt quote. Whatever it was, as Tom and I walked into the glittering room, I felt, for the first time in a long time, that I was exactly where I was supposed to be. Despite the snowy white table cloths adorned with a glittering array of silver and crystal and giant flower arrangements lit by soft candlelight – all of which might have made me uncomfortable at one time – it felt absolutely right.

What Tom hadn't told me was that he was the host and master of ceremonies, which meant that we'd be sitting at a dazzling head table with six city luminaries. I watched him with nothing short of admiration as he deftly greeted people and introduced each speaker with humour and self-effacement.

After the dinner, a band set up on a small stage.

"Would you care to dance?" Tom said, offering me his hand.

I wasn't much of a dancer, but at that moment, there was nothing I wanted more.

~

When the evening came to an end, and Tom kissed me goodnight (yes, he kissed me!) I think I knew what Cinderella had felt like after the ball. I undressed and put an old robe on. I went to the kitchen to pour myself a glass of water. I sat for a moment at the red Formica table that was still there and gazed out the window remembering how wonderful it had felt this evening. My phone was sitting on the table. I picked it up and absently scrolled through my email. There was one from a vaguely familiar sender. I clicked on it.

"Dear Ms. Hudson:

I hope this email finds you well. You might remember our conversation last year when we discussed the possibility of you joining the faculty at Princess Margaret College. I realize that you had decided against this move at that time, but I am hoping that your circumstances might have changed, and you might once again consider us.

As you know, we were impressed by your academic background and your feature writing, as well as your ability to present your ideas at the interview.

We still believe that you would be an asset to the school and our students. If this possibility intrigues you, please call my office so that we can once again discuss the possibility of you joining us. We have a need for you in January and will need your decision by December 1.

With warm regards, Devin Connors, Headmaster, Princess Margaret College."

There was only one thing I knew for sure at that moment: sleeping was going to be a challenge.

November

I always used to think of November as the darkest month of the year, but somehow, this year, everything seemed different. When the first of November rolled around a few days after my "date" with Tom, I should have been worried about where I was going to live, how I was going to pay the rent, whether or not my fall jacket was warm enough for those increasingly cold mornings, the actual location of my favourite gloves and the list goes on. But I wasn't. It didn't even faze me that morning when I opened my blinds to see – snow! It was far too early in our neck of the woods for snow, but there it was – a light coating of white as if Mother Nature had shaken out a clean white sheet and laid it over the dreary dead grass and the naked tree branches. I was delighted. Although to tell you the truth, I really did have no idea where my gloves were, and I was certainly going to need them.

I showered and dressed slowly, then sipped my coffee as if in slow motion. It was only when my phone pinged with a reminder that I realized today was the day Miss Davies had said she'd tell me the rest of the story. How could I have forgotten? Did it have anything to do with how mawkishly besotted I'd become with Tom? Just maybe. Oh, and what about the email from that private school? I was still avoiding it two days later, but in my defence, it was the weekend. I'd get to it next week.

I had never been inside Miss Davies's house other than in the basement studio. When I turned into the walkway as I had done several months ago, I felt a sudden jolt of wistfulness for what might have been. In retrospect, though, it seemed clear to me that I was meant to be in the old house for just a bit longer. It still didn't help with my increasingly dire housing situation.

I walked up the three front steps as I had done on my first visit and knocked. Miss Davies came to the door. I was surprised at her outfit. She was wearing jeans and what looked like a cashmere sweater. Why I had expected that someone of her vintage (over seventy) would be wearing some version of a housedress was beyond me. I had seen Mae Musk (Elon's dietitian-turned-model mother) in all her seventy-plus glory peering out from the pages of fashion magazines. And my mother certainly didn't dress like an old matronly grandmother, although she did tend toward the uptight, tailored look as I've mentioned. But Miss Davies was a spinster (does anyone use that word anymore?) and probably had cats, or at least that's what I thought. I only hoped that there'd be no doilies on the chairs. I think I have a doily phobia. I was wrong about her in so many ways I can't even count them.

Miss Davies pushed a stray silver hair off her forehead as she led me into the living room. I noticed that she was a tiny woman – she couldn't have been any more than about five-feet-two, and preternaturally thin, notwithstanding her resemblance to Dame Judi. She had seemed so much larger outside her home. I was wrong about the cats. Sitting in a chair set beside a very modern gas fireplace was an adorable King Charles spaniel. The minute he saw me, he got up from his comfortable perch and wandered over, amiably wagging his tail.

"Meet Jethro," Miss Davies said as she gestured for me to sit down on one of the two cushy love seats that faced one another across a marble-topped coffee table.

I sank into the most comfortable sofa I'd ever experienced and nestled into three poshly-covered toss pillows. I love dogs, so I was happy to find that Jethro seemed to like me. When Miss Davies started to shoo him away, I told her I didn't mind a bit. So, Jethro snuggled up against me, burrowing in against my leg. It was a lovely feeling.

She checked her watch. "Only four p.m., but I think we're going to need something a bit stronger than coffee. Martini?"

Another surprise. Of course, a martini would be excellent. Miss Davies went to a bar set up beside the fireplace and removed two martini glasses from a bar fridge I hadn't noticed since it was built into the cupboards below the bar. She expertly mixed two martinis, popped olives into the glasses, poured and served.

"Given the circumstances, Charlotte, I think you can call me Elizabeth."

"Only if you call me Charlie," I said, sipping the exquisite martini with just a hint of vermouth. Just the way I liked them.

"Charlie it is, then." She took up a position on the loveseat across the marble expanse from me and put her glass on one of the wooden coasters laid out on the coffee table. She bent down and withdrew a red metal box that had been hidden beneath the coffee table then settled back, drawing her legs up under her.

At the sight of the box, I froze with my glass just inches away from my lips and stopped breathing for a few seconds. What did she have in that box? Did I really want to know? Then I breathed out and mentally slapped myself up the side of the head. Of course, I wanted to know. And there could be nothing about my mother that I'd prefer not to know.

She opened the box and put it on the sofa beside her then leaned over to take a sip of her drink. "Before I tell you about your mother, Charlie, I'd love to know about you."

"Me? Whatever for?"

"Because, Charlie darling, you're a lot like your mother. I first noticed it the second day you were in my class back in junior high school. You had a wide-eyed wonder about new things – about the world."

"Miss Davies...Elizabeth, that doesn't describe my mother at all. In fact, my sister Evelyn who you might also remember from a couple of years before me has always been more like Mom. I mean, Mom was so perfect. She was always the perfect mother, teacher, wife. She always had her head on straight. I always had my head in the clouds."

"You're a writer, aren't you?"

I nodded. "Sort of. At least it's my passion. I truly love writing. I haven't honestly been able to make much of a living at it, though." I sipped my drink.

She nodded her head slightly. "So, you're the artist?"

"I guess so."

"You don't seem so sure of yourself."

"I suppose I'm at one of those personal watersheds in life. I'm trying desperately to be on the path I'm passionate about, but I seem to be spinning my wheels."

"Before your mother died, did she ever tell you to stop pursuing your writing?"

Mom had never once told me to reconsider my choice to pursue writing. She had never once told me to get a real job. She had always been in my corner. Evelyn, on the other hand, had started on me the minute I applied to study creative writing in grad school. I told Elizabeth all this.

"Would it surprise you to know that before your mother met your father, she was on a path to an artistic career?"

Would it surprise me? Surprise didn't even come close. Disbelief or shock might have edged closer.

"She had just finished her second year at the Parsons School in New York when that photo you have of her at Woodstock was taken."

And my mind immediately snapped. The Parsons School. The Parsons School of *Design.* Pre-eminent, private American college offering, among other things, graphic design, interior design and fashion design. The alma mater of the likes of Donna Karan, Marc Jacobs, Anna Sui and the list goes on. I choked a little on my drink.

"And Mom studied –"

"You know," Elizabeth said, looking at me steadily. "Why do you think she had a sewing machine? And all those patterns? And this." She pulled a notebook from the box and gave it to me.

I placed my glass on the coaster closest to me and took it from her. I sat back and began thumbing through it. My mother's maiden name was emblazoned in broad, loud strokes on the front. Inside were meticulously created sketches of every kind of clothing you can imagine. Shirts, sweaters, pants, coats, blazers, cocktail dresses. It went on and on, each of the sketches displaying a specific style, a specific aesthetic. It took my breath away.

"This belonged to my mother?"

"It not only belonged to her but was created by her. It might be difficult for you to believe this, but your mother was poised to become one of the hottest fashion designers of her age. All her professors told her that. And I thought so, too."

"Why…?"

"Why did she never tell you and your sister about this?" I nodded. It was all I could do. "I might have some insight into that." Then she told me a story.

The world was a different place in the 1960s. I knew that. I had read about the "swinging sixties," but it had never really meant anything to me beyond being something for the history books. I guess I knew that Mom and Dad had lived through that era, but it was probably a bit like their own parents telling them about World War II. Important historically but somehow illusory, as much of history appears to school children. Like everyone else in my generation, I had always just accepted the stories as historical fact – or myth in the case of Woodstock – not as a part of my own family's heritage. I had never considered my parents and how they might have been different people all those years ago. Miss Davies – Elizabeth – set me straight.

"I met your mother two years before she went to Parsons. I was in my second year at the University of Toronto," she began. They were both from the same home town but had gone to different high schools, so they had never met before enrolling at U of T. Both of them had been studying to be teachers when they met. Mom was majoring in English with a minor in history. Elizabeth was a food science major who would later finish her home economics studies to include textiles and sewing back home at a university on the east coast.

"We bonded immediately. We had compatible interests, similar senses of humour. We studied together, shopped together on Yonge Street, listened to music at the Yorkville coffeehouses. Your mother was such a folkie! She would have dragged me out to Yorkville coffeehouses every evening if I'd let her!" She smiled at the memory.

My mother liked folk music? How could this be possible? The only music I ever saw around our house were stacks of classical DVDs and some jazz.

"And, oh, the bars!" she continued. "It was a wonderful time to be young! We had two years together –sharing a dorm room – before your mother dropped out when she was offered a scholarship to Parsons. She never really wanted to be a teacher, you know. But your grandparents had discouraged her from pursuing her design dreams."

The fact that Mom had dropped out of the University of Toronto was a complete revelation to me on top of everything else. I didn't even know she had ever been a student there. That's not what the teaching degree she had finally received had said. I had seen her parchment. But facing her parents' discouragement? "So, she defied them?"

"You could say that. She didn't tell them she was applying to Parsons, and she didn't tell them when we hitchhiked across the border so she could do the interview and portfolio presentation in person." Elizabeth picked up both our glasses – now empty – and took them to the bar for a refill. She passed me a fresh drink and sat back down again, pulling her legs up underneath her again as a young teenager might do.

"You went with her?"

"Of course. I wouldn't have missed a chance to go to New York City for anything. It was magical." A wistfulness seemed to pass over her eyes for a split second. "While we were there, she met Charles Cohen – Chuck."

According to Elizabeth, Chuck was a third-year photography student at Parsons, who Mom literally ran into in the corridor on her way to her appointment. As she later told Elizabeth the story, she was in such a hurry that she knocked one of his precious cameras right out of his hands. When she was finished her interview, he was waiting for her in the hall. He apparently wanted to take some photos of her.

"She was skeptical, but she told him if he'd include her friend – me – that she'd agree. I guess she thought she'd be safe with me along in case he turned out to be a wacko of some sort." She laughed. "He wasn't a wacko. What he turned out to be was in madly love with your mother – after only one weekend."

I choked on my drink. "I guess that explains the way he was looking at her in those pictures. So, I guess they made a plan to meet at Woodstock?"

"In a manner of speaking, but a lot more happened before that. This was 1967. Woodstock happened two years later."

Mom received her acceptance letter to Parsons in June of 1967, along with the offer of a substantial scholarship. Given the exorbitant cost of education at this prestigious school, it was the only way she would have been able to go. That's when she finally told her parents – my Grama and Grandad. Both of them had died when I was a teenager, but I remembered them as being stern and a bit sour. I had never gotten a warm and fuzzy feeling from my grandparents – especially my grandfather– so I could only imagine what Mom must have faced when she told them about it. According to what Mom later told Elizabeth, they had been less negative about it than she had expected, especially when she waved the scholarship letter in front of them. They, however, had been very negative when she brought Chuck home to meet them that summer before classes started.

"

"The summer before your mother left for New York, Chuck came up to visit. Your mother was crazy about him. Your grandparents were decidedly not."

"What was wrong with him?"

Elizabeth looked at me. "Among other things, he was Jewish."

"What? What difference would that have made?"

"Your mother hadn't thought it would make any difference. It seemed that your grandparents harboured, not so much anti-Semitism as anti-anything that wasn't white-Anglo-Saxon-Protestant and exactly like them. It was fine to have friends and acquaintances of all cultures and faiths, but you didn't get intimately involved. It wasn't done in their circles. And we can be as self-righteous as we want here in the twenty-first century, but that's just the way it was then. They were polite to him while he was there, then they forbade her to ever see him again."

"So, I'm guessing that didn't go down well with Mom."

According to Elizabeth, a major fight ensued. It seems that my grandparents – at least my grandfather – actually forbade her to accept the scholarship and go to New York. My mother defied them and went anyway.

Elizabeth then took several letters from the red box and passed them to me. "You should have these."

I looked at the envelopes. "They're from Mom to you." She nodded. "They're private."

"You should have them, Charlie. When you read them, you'll see how much she loved Chuck – and you'll understand the events that followed."

"Why did you save them?"

"I think when you read them, you'll understand. I couldn't bear to destroy the only remaining evidence of such a love." Then she went on with her story.

When Mom and Chuck first heard about plans for a music festival in upstate New York in early 1969, they managed to convince Elizabeth and her then-boyfriend to make plans to come to New York in August and go upstate to the festival with them. When they made this decision, they had no idea that this would be such a massive gathering – or that it would enter the annals of history as one of those watershed moments in youth culture.

"You know we actually each bought copy of *Cheap Thrills*, Janis Joplin's last album she did with Big

Brother and the Holding Company so that we could bone up on psychedelic rock music before we went. We didn't want to seem like squares. I think I still have mine."

It was clear Mom still didn't have hers. I would have found it. And what would Dad have thought, anyway? "You and Mom weren't fans?"

Elizabeth shook her head. "Not really. We were more into Simon and Garfunkel, Crosby, Stills and Nash, Joan Baez. That kind of music. We knew that there would be our kind of music there, but we wanted to know more about Janis, Jimi Hendrix – sort of psychedelic rock music – before we went."

"What was it like being there?"

"It was incredible," Elizabeth said as she reached inside the box to retrieve some photos. "And since Chuck was a photographer, we ended up with amazing pictures, some of which he published later."

She passed me one of the photos. I looked at it and saw my mother's beaming face staring out into the world. She had her arm around another young woman with wild hair and a pair of round, dark-tinted granny glasses half-way down her nose. She looked vaguely familiar.

"Please don't tell me you don't know who that is," Elizabeth almost pleaded with me. I shrugged. She shook her head. "It's Janis Joplin."

"I know that name," I said, pretending ignorance. She rolled her eyes, and I laughed. "I'm joking. And I'm impressed. I do know who Janis Joplin was. But the question is, how in the world did my mother end up in a photo with her?" This was seriously mind-blowing.

"Chuck had his ways. He knew a lot of people. One of them happened to be one of Janis's guitarists. She had a new band by then. I think it was called the Kosmic Blues Band or something like that. Anyway, her first performance was at something like two or three o'clock in the morning. The next day Chuck arranged for us to go backstage and meet some of the musicians. I remember observing that most of them were stoned out of their minds." She stopped as if she could see the scene in her mind's eye. "Looking back, I suppose Janis was, too, but she seemed to be able to handle it. Anyway, it seemed that your mother and Janis Joplin shared a birthday."

"January 19, 1946," I said. I might not have known when Janis Joplin, rock legend, was born, but I did know my own mother's birthdate. It seemed it might have been one of the few things I did know about her.

"Well, the same date, different year. Janis was actually born in 1943, but she was childishly delighted to find what she called her long-lost twin sister who shared the same January birthday. It was quite a moment in time. It was only after Woodstock that things got a bit strange."

Elizabeth and her boyfriend had returned to Canada. Elizabeth started teaching what was, at that time, still home economics. She taught junior high school girls sewing, cooking and family studies. By all accounts, she loved her job. But by early October of 1969, she knew that something was terribly wrong. She was pregnant.

"Your mother, being the wonderful friend that she was, made arrangements for me to have an abortion in New York. And no, it wasn't actually legal, but New York state was working to make abortion legal at that time – which it did the next year – so there were already private clinics quietly preparing for the change in the law. Your mother found me one. That way, no one here at home would ever find out. I'd just be off sick for a week and then go back to work. I drove to New York, had the abortion at a clinic. While I was there, Chuck received his draft notice. He was going to Vietnam. Your mother was crazed with fright and anger. He told her he'd be fine and that they'd get married when he returned."

"Why didn't Mom suggest they move to Canada? There were lots of guys who avoided the draft by coming here."

"She did suggest it. In fact, she told me that she begged him. But Chuck thought he'd miss an opportunity to build his career by proving himself a talented war photographer if he could take photos in the field." Elizabeth's face seemed to soften into a remote sadness. "He was the young man in the combat helmet in the photo."

He never returned. Mom descended into a deep depression to the point where she couldn't even go to class. When they heard that Chuck had died, her parents welcomed her back with open arms. She dropped out of Parsons, spent six months recovering at my grandparents' home then went back to a local university to finish her teaching degree.

"She was so ill from all of this that we didn't see one another for those six months. She didn't see anyone."

My mind was reeling from the revelations, but there was still one detail that I didn't understand. "If you two were such close friends for so long, what happened? Why did Mom never mention that she even knew you?"

"That would be my fault," Elizabeth said. "I suppose I hoped I wouldn't have to tell you this, but I think you deserve the whole story." She rearranged her legs and grabbed a cushion, which she hugged to herself as if to protect her from what was coming. "When I first mentioned to you that we'd been in Woodstock, I told you that we'd listened to music, smoked dope and –"

"Made love," I finished her sentence. "Or at least there was a lot of sex as far as I can make out."

"Yes," she said, hesitating before continuing. "We listened to lots of music, and did smoke a lot of dope."

This astounded me. I mean, an old spinster, and my mom? I kept forgetting that they were no more than twenty-two or three at the time, young, beautiful and carefree, both of them. Why was it so hard to get my head around the fact that my mother had a life before parenthood? Why did children have such a hard time seeing their parents as people?

Elizabeth continued. "And we did make love with whoever was around." She stopped again. "After your mother recovered somewhat and returned to university to complete her degree, we started spending time together again. One evening we decided to go bar-hopping and ended up having far too much to drink. She started sobbing about Chuck. And about me having to have an abortion and how sorry she'd been about the fact I'd had to make such a hard decision. In my inebriation, I started talking and told her the truth about the baby."

"It was Chuck's, wasn't it?" I said, now understanding things clearly.

She nodded. "Your mother never forgave me. She didn't even come to my wedding."

I sat up abruptly.

"You didn't know I'd been married, did you? It's not really 'Miss' Davies," she said. "It's Mrs. Davies. My husband died in a car crash a year after we were married, and I never found anyone else I wanted to share my life with – except, of course, Jethro."

Jethro was fast asleep on the sofa beside me. "I'm so sorry," I said. "I had no idea."

"You know," she said, hugging the cushion closer to her chest, "when you're young, you think you'll never be any older than you are in that moment. The truth is that you'll never be that young again."

A lump started forming in my throat. I looked at Miss Davies and didn't quite know how I felt about her now. I was beginning to understand that we all live many different lives – all in one lifetime.

~

Evelyn had stopped calling and texting as often since the house sale closed. I suppose that other than connecting with her younger sister, there was nothing more she needed to needle me about. And truthfully, I wasn't as good a sounding board for marital troubles as her therapist. I had no idea where she and Michael were on their relationship trajectory. I did realize, however, that I'd have to tell her Mom's story at some point. I wasn't quite ready yet, though.

I was still reeling from Miss Davies's story, and reading Mom's letters describing her life and love with

Chuck didn't help. I sat in bed that evening reading and sobbing. I was wishing that I'd know my mother better when she was alive. I was wishing that she was here to tell me about it herself. I was wishing she had trusted her daughters enough to share it. I was wishing that she had told me about her design passion. I think, most of all, I was wishing I'd appreciated her unwavering support for my artistic pursuits more. I needed to say thank-you. But she was gone.

This was still on my mind the next morning as I pushed my library cart through the stacks, reading spines and replacing books in their well-ordered spaces. Libraries were so much more orderly than lives were. Lives were messy.

It was still on my mind when I pushed open the door at *Sew Fine Things* later that afternoon. Al was his usual cheerful self, but I noted that he seemed a bit distracted. When I pulled my patterns out of my backpack, he smiled, but at the same time, glanced down at his phone, which was on the counter beside him. He seemed to be waiting for a call.

"Charlie, these are good choices for you." He picked up a pattern for a sheath dress with a lovely swing-style jacket. "This one."

"Yeah, that looks simple enough." I was looking at the lines of the sleeveless dress and knew that I could handle it.

"But not just the dress," he said, reaching for a bolt of what looked to me like the kind of tweed you might see in a Chanel advertisement. You know the ones. Those jackets. "You need to make both pieces."

I wasn't at all sure about making a jacket, but I was willing to give it a try. Then I started thinking about how I regretted not telling Mom how much her support over the years had meant even if my writing career was going nowhere. I told Al just a tiny bit about the fact that Mom had been a budding designer. Thinking that it might interest him, I had brought Mom's sketchbook along. I now took it out of my backpack and offered it to him.

He took it from me and began to turn the pages one after the other. He whistled softly. "Your mother, she was very talented," he said. "Now I can see where you got your artistic streak."

"I wish I had told her how much her support meant to me. Now I'll never get a chance."

He closed the sketchbook and passed it back to me. "I think she probably knew," he said. "Parents are intuitive that way."

"Maybe."

"Do you know what John F. Kennedy said about gratitude?"

I did not.

"'*As we express our gratitude, we must never forget that the highest appreciation is not to utter the words but to live by them.*'"

I smiled. And I knew what to do.

~

The November meeting of my writers' group was just getting underway. I was excited to share my writing this month, a feeling I hadn't had in a very long time. There was something I had to say to them. But after I'd unwrapped my scarf and hung up my heavy coat in Joseph's hall closet, it was clear that whatever I might have to say this evening would have to take second place. Karl had news.

As I walked into the living room, I discovered Karl pouring champagne into crystal flutes that Joseph naturally owned for special occasions.

"Charlie," Karl said as I walked in, "come. Join us in a glass of champagne."

"Of course," I said, reaching for the flute he held out to me. "What are we celebrating?"

Miriam, looking only slightly less sour than usual, piped up from the chair where she was ensconced, her voluminous, wildly-coloured caftan spread out around her. “It appears Karl has news.” Did she do a slight eye roll? “He has not shared it as yet.”

I sat down on the sofa with Wendy, who was sipping contentedly on champagne. (How was it that she’d arrived before me again?) Joseph took up the chair beside Miriam and gestured to Karl. “The floor is yours.”

Karl stood and raised his glass. “First, I want to toast all of you, my writing colleagues. I want to thank you for all the feedback you’ve given me over the years. You’ve made me a better writer.”

Where was this going? I felt my stomach do a little drop. I was as aware as the next person that everything comes to an end, but if Karl was leaving the group, I wasn’t sure I could continue.

“Oh, get on with it,” Joseph said excitedly as if he might already be in on whatever it was.

“I’ve sold a book!”

There was a second of silence as we all processed this. Then, I placed my glass on the table and began clapping. Wendy immediately joined in, then Joseph started clapping. We all stood up. Miriam was a bit late with the clapping and had difficulty getting to her feet but eventually joined us. We hugged Karl and shook his hand. This was what every writer works toward. It’s an achievement that every single one of us in the room was hoping would happen. To us.

Karl's eyes were shining, and not from too much champagne. I knew he wasn't much of a drinker.

"I suppose you'll be leaving our little group in search of a group of published writers such as yourself?" Miriam's enthusiasm for this announcement seemed a bit muted in comparison to the rest of us.

As much as I wished for the same outcome, I didn't begrudge Karl or any other aspiring writer for that matter, such success. These days, we can all publish our own work, but this kind of acknowledgement from a publisher, who is willing to put their money where their mouth is, is quite a coup. I was aware, however, that Miriam's quasi-disdain probably emanated not from jealousy (although that was probably a factor) but from her condescending attitude toward the kind of writing Karl was passionate about – romance novels. I decided it was best to ignore her and focus on Karl.

"So, Karl, did you finally come up with a pen name for the books, or will it just be Karl?"

He smiled. "I thought about being Karl, but in the end, after discussions with my publisher, and my wife," he laughed, "we decided that I'd be Karli Lake."

"Bravo, Karli. I love it!" I said, sipping on my champagne.

Miriam snorted. "Yes, well done, Karl." She sat down, arranged her drapes around her and took up her champagne. "So, shall we read now?"

Everyone nodded. "I'll start," I said, an eventuality that I'm quite sure surprised everyone there. I hadn't offered to go first for a very long time, but I had a date with Tom later and wanted to be sure I got this story off my chest. And so, I began. It was a short story about a writers' group with five members, all different. Each member had something unique to offer the others. When I reached the end, everyone was still listening, which was a good thing. I ended the story with something Albert Einstein once said. "*There are only two ways to live your life. One is as though nothing is a miracle. The other is as though everything is a miracle.*"

I looked around at my four friends, each one as different as night and day but all people to whom I owed a debt of gratitude. "Thank-you for being part of my miracle."

December

"Finish it."

There it was again. That little whisper haunting me. In my head, it sounded like it might be Mom calling to me. But I knew that it was my own little voice. It's that voice in everybody's head that you ignore at your peril. My problem was that I still had so many unfinished matters, it could refer to almost anything.

This was on my mind when I awoke on the first of December. I had left things unfinished with my writers' group. After I thanked them all for what they'd shared with me over the years, there seemed to be a great, big elephant in the room. With Karl's clear move forward in his publishing career and my thanking everyone like you might do when you're retiring or something, that elephant loomed. Was the group ready to disband – finish – or was it going to be able to continue with the changed dynamic? I wasn't at all certain that I was the one who had to finish this. My only decision was whether or not it was over for *me*.

Then there was the ongoing matter of my novel-in-progress. I had chosen one of my unfinished manuscripts – the one I seemed to like the best – and gotten back to work on it. I was moving forward slowly, but I couldn't see even a glimmer of light at the end of the tunnel. And it wasn't the only finish line that was murky, either.

This morning, there were two matters of unfinished business that were taking priority over all else. I had two deadlines looming, and I had to meet both of them before the end of the day.

As I opened the blinds, I started to laugh. There in front of me was another cloak of newly-fallen snow. My bedroom window looked out into the backyard, where the unblemished mantle of white sparkled in the morning sunshine. It was as if a sack of tiny diamonds had been spilled into the yard overnight. Its simple perfection somehow made me feel as if I were beginning some new and exciting adventure. Here I'd been considering endings, but what I really needed to focus on was beginnings. Because if I'd learned anything this past year, it was that everything that ended meant that something new was about to begin. It was time I got on with it.

I showered and dressed quickly. As I sat eating a bowl of shredded wheat with skim milk (I had decided that I needed to step up my eating habits to those of an adult) and sipping a cup of coffee, I was considering the two pieces of paper on the table. The piece of paper beside my right elbow was from the landlord of a small apartment building where I'd found a charming little one-bedroom that I actually liked. It was in a nice part of town and was well-kept with its front courtyard filled with trees, and tenants who seemed to be older people rather than students. It was time for me to be in a more adult environment, I thought. I had to let him know today if I was going to take it. I would move in on January first, which seemed to me to be appropriate.

At my left elbow was a print-out of that email I'd received a month ago from Devin Connors, Headmaster at that private high school, Princess Margaret College. I'd spoken with him on the telephone twice since the email arrived, and now he was expecting a final call from me today. I had thought long and hard about this one. It had so many implications for my life – past, present and future. I'd discussed it with Tom, whose approach was to ask me a few pointed questions and then let me persuade myself one way or another. Now that I thought about our conversations on the matter, he had not once offered an opinion. It was entirely up to me, and he wasn't going to influence my decision. I'd thought of it from as many angles as I could and was now exhausted. At least I had exhausted every pro and con I could think of. All that was left was to decide.

I hadn't breathed a single word about this to Evelyn. I thought I'd wait until I'd made a decision before conferring with her. It had been difficult for me to hold my tongue when she called last week to invite me to spend Christmas in Toronto. It seemed that she and Michael had decided to reconcile after a short separation of a month when Michael had moved in with a friend while Evelyn stewed alone in the condo and threw herself into her work for fourteen-hour days. Whenever I thought about her invitation, I felt slightly nauseous. What could be worse than spending Christmas stuck between two sullen adults who were trying to work through relationship issues? Certainly, spending Christmas alone packing up for a move would be preferable, wouldn't it? Anyway, I still had to let her know. I felt as if I were juggling balls that were in serious jeopardy of falling.

Well, there was no time like the present to get rid of one of those balls. I picked up the paper on my right about the apartment and checked the telephone number. I was just about to tap the first number when my phone started vibrating in my hand. It was Tom calling.

"Charlie! You still at home?"

"Yes. I'm just about to call that landlord and let him know I'll take the apartment. I'm kind of excited about it, too."

"Can you wait five minutes before you call him?"

"I suppose I could. Why?"

"Five minutes." And he hung up.

This was all a bit too mysterious so early in the morning. I looked at the time on my telephone. I could wait five minutes.

Less than a minute later, the doorbell rang. When I opened the door, Tom was standing there on the porch, dangling a key in front of him.

"Good morning, Charlie."

"Good morning, Tom." I looked past him and saw his car parked at the curb. "You called from your car?"

"I did." He dangled a bit more enthusiastically. "See this?"

I nodded. It was clearly a key.

"Do you know what it is?"

"Tom, it's a key. That much is clear."

"May I come in?"

I let him in, and we went directly to the kitchen, where I made him a cup of coffee. He didn't speak until we were both sitting down opposite one another at the red Formica table I'd decided I had to take with me to my new apartment.

"Here's the thing, Charlie," he said, clearing his throat. He had placed the key on the table between us. Now he picked it up and looked at it. "The thing is...well, the thing is that this is a key to my house."

"Okay," I said slowly.

"I'd like it to be *your* key to my house." As I processed this oddity, he continued. "Because I'd like you to move in with me. You know how well we get along with one another. I think we're uber compatible." He took my hand and put the key into it. "That's not right. I think we're more than compatible. The truth is, Charlie, I love you."

My head felt as if it might explode. I knew I loved Tom. I had from almost that first moment when he came to the door all those months ago. And he was right – we were *more* than compatible – but I hadn't been certain about his feelings. Until now. But moving in with him?

Tom lived in a beautifully restored Victorian mansion in a grand old neighbourhood of equally beautiful restored homes. In fact, it wasn't that far from where Miss Davies – Elizabeth – lived. He'd bought the house after he sold his internet business and was very proud of it. I remember how proud he'd seemed as he showed me around the place, pointing out to me the little touches he'd added himself. Touches like the wall sconces in the hallway and the inlay in the floor in his den. But could I live there? I suddenly realized that I could live anywhere if it was with Tom.

I closed my hand around the key.

Tom looked down at the paper from the landlord. "You'll tell him no, right?" His eyes were bright.

"I'll tell him no."

That left one more deadline for today.

~

Tom and I made a plan to have dinner at his place that evening, then he left to show a house. We were both as giddy as a couple of pre-teen girls hovering over a makeup counter at Sephora. I was beginning to get the sense of what a new beginning feels like and realized that it had been a very long time since I'd felt it. I liked it. But it didn't mean that I had to blow up my entire life. Next on the agenda was that other piece of paper. The email from Devin Connors.

I walked into the living room and sat down at the sewing machine. "Tell me what to do," I said. As usual, Junior didn't respond. I picked up two patterns that were lying on top of one of the pattern boxes and thought, *This one would be terrific for teaching a class.* Then I picked up another one. Could I learn to sew pants, I wondered? This one would look great at the front of a classroom, too. But making this kind of change would be a whole lot more than changing wardrobe choices. It was a career choice. A new direction.

I turned and looked at the large, flat cardboard box that had been lingering on the floor for months since Evelyn and I had opened it up and wondered what it was. It suddenly struck me that Miss Davies –

Elizabeth – might know what it was supposed to be. I walked back into the kitchen where I'd left my phone and the key to my new home. I smiled as I tapped Elizabeth's number while ignoring the email from Mr. Connors.

"Well, hello, Charlie. I hope things are going well for you. You're moving soon, are you not?"

"Hello…Elizabeth. Yes, I'm getting ready to move out of the old house." I was still having some trouble not calling her Miss Davies. "I was wondering if you might be able to help me identify one more thing that was obviously my mother's. I guess I need to figure out if I should keep it or not."

"I'd be happy to help you if I can."

"I think it might be easiest if you saw it. I could bring it over."

"Why don't I drop in to see it? I was just getting ready to go out for a walk with Jethro. If you don't mind a dog in the house, I could walk in your direction. It's such a lovely snowy day, but I fear the snow is rapidly melting with this sun!"

Elizabeth arrived forty-five minutes later, and I still had not called Mr. Connors. It could wait until after I had this mystery sorted out. Then that would be one more bit of unfinished business off my plate.

After Elizabeth had gotten her coat and boots off and Jethro had greeted me happily, he settled in a sunbeam in the living room while I placed the box on the sewing machine table and opened it.

The moment I opened it and the contents were visible, Elizabeth walked over and started touching the lace. She lifted the first piece from the box and began to lay it out on the floor as I had done.

Then she placed another piece, and another. She knew exactly where each of the puzzle pieces fit. She said nothing as she arranged them. When she had finished, and all of the pieces were laid out on the floor, I saw a tear escape her left eye and roll down her cheek. She lifted her hand to wipe it away.

"Oh my, Charlie," she said. "I haven't seen this since 1970."

"The year after Woodstock." She nodded. "Then it *was* my mother's?"

"Yes," she said quietly. "It was Kat's."

"I know it's a dress cut out, but what was it for?"

Elizabeth crossed her arms as if to warm herself up, then placed one hand on her mouth. "It was meant to be her wedding gown."

I was puzzled. "But Mom and Dad didn't get married until 1976. They didn't even know each other then, as far as I know."

She looked at me sadly. And I knew.

"It wasn't for Mom's wedding to Dad, was it?"

She shook her head. "She and Chuck had planned to be married the moment he returned from Vietnam. I was visiting her in New York when she bought the fabric. We had such a wonderful day exploring the garment district." Elizabeth had a faraway look in her eyes. "She told me that she wanted her dress to be perfect and to be ready for the moment he returned so that the wedding wouldn't be delayed by anything."

"She never finished it," I said, sitting down cross-legged on the floor beside the pieces of the dress. "He was killed before she even had a chance to finish it, wasn't he?" And at that moment, I wondered if Dad had been her second choice for all those years.

"Yes. I'm surprised that she kept it. I thought she'd fling it into the garbage in one of her depressions that year. Then I never thought about it again." Elizabeth sat down beside me.

We sat in silence for a few moments. Jethro turned over and repositioned himself. I now knew it was time I told Evelyn about Mom. And Chuck.

After Elizabeth left, I stood looking over the fabric pieces I'd left laid out on the floor where she had put them and tried to picture Mom in the finished dress. But the image wouldn't come.

"*Finish it.*"

The voice was so clear this time. And there was no more ambiguity. I knew what had to be finished.

~

It was time. I'd cleaned up my lunch dishes and convinced myself that I'd given Devin Connors enough time to finish his lunch. I had to call. It was now or never.

"Hello, Ms. Hudson." His voice boomed through my phone. "Delighted to hear from you. Tell me that you have good news."

"I hope it's good news, Mr. Connors." I cleared my throat. "First, I want to thank you for offering me this wonderful opportunity. As you know, I've had to think long and hard about how this move would change my career path and my writing."

"That's one of the reasons we want you here at Princess Margaret. I'd like to think that our offer might provide that clear path."

"You know, Mr. Connors, I think it just might. I cannot think of any place I'd rather be in January than standing in front of a class of your students sharing with them my love of writing."

"Then it's final. You'll join us in January?"

"I will."

"Ms. Hudson, I hope that you will gain as much from this as I know our students will gain from you."

I was fairly certain that I'd be the big winner here.

We made arrangements for me to touch base with their human resources director then he wished me a happy festive season and hung up. I sat in the kitchen for a few minutes taking a bit of time to consider what I'd just done. Another beginning. But was it an ending, too? Most beginnings started with endings. Was this the end of my journey to be a writer, or would I be able to continue it? Did I even want to? That remained to be seen.

~

It was going to be a busy month. I had to get my belongings and the rest of what remained in Mom's house sorted and packed. I sat down at my computer to make a list of the things I'd have to do. When I was finished, I looked at it on the screen and wondered if I'd get through it all in time. Then I realized that I'd been able to successfully clear out the house so I ought to be able to finish the rest of the jobs, the most important of which made its way under the needle of my sewing machine three days after Elizabeth told me it was my mother's.

When I first approached the pieces of fabric, each one I picked up seemed imbued with Mom's spirit, a spirit I now knew was a flame that burned much brighter back when she first decided on the pattern and fabric and laid it out to cut out the pieces. I wondered what she'd been thinking about as she pinned the pattern on and cut out each piece. As I put the first two pieces of fabric under the needle, I took a deep breath. I couldn't screw this up. There was no extra fabric. It had to be right. I could almost feel Mom around me. And I felt her smiling over my shoulder. I stepped on the pedal and was off.

I worked on the dress for three solid days. I couldn't seem to let it go once it started coming together. At the end of the third day, as I put the last hand-stitch into the hem, I realized that I didn't want it to end. I didn't want the story to be over. I didn't want it to be finished. But it was. I put it on one of the padded hangers I found in Mom's closet early in the year and hung it up on the door to my bedroom. I sat on the bed and looked at it.

I was proud of myself, and I thought Mom would have been proud if she could have seen it. I lifted the hanger down and held the dress in front of me and looked down. I walked over to the full-length mirror and looked at myself, holding the dress up, seeing the folds of white lace drape around my legs. Before I could stop myself, I was pulling off my jeans and my sweater and climbing into the dress. I twisted myself so that I could pull up the invisible zipper I'd put into the back of it, then I stood up and once again looked into the mirror.

Staring back at me was – Mom. I had never before really seen the resemblance Evelyn talked about, but it was unmistakable. And the dress was a perfect fit. This is what Mom would have looked like back all those years ago on the day she would have been married. I tried to squeeze my eyes closed to keep the tears that were threatening to emerge from spilling down my cheeks. I was unsuccessful.

I was so intent on trying not to cry that I didn't hear the back door open. I didn't hear the footsteps coming down the hallway toward my bedroom, and I didn't see anyone standing in the bedroom door.

"Charlie!" Evelyn shrieked. "What in the world are you wearing?"

I was so startled I almost tripped on the long folds of the dress. I caught myself just in time.

"Evelyn, what are you doing here?"

"I wanted to talk to you. I can see that there might be quite a lot you need to tell me."

She had no idea.

"Help me out of this," I said, trying to unzip myself from the white lace. I must have looked peculiar indeed to my older sister, who, by the way, I noted looked better than she had in months. Her hair was once again glossy and straight. Her eyes seemed to be shining when they weren't clouded by confusion as I began to tell her the story Elizabeth had told me.

I hung the dress in my closet and took Evelyn to the kitchen. "We're going to need a drink for this," I said.

"I'd really like a coffee first," she said. So, I made coffee then we settled in to talk.

Two hours later, I'd managed to tell her the whole story. She was speechless.

"Well, it explains what those fabric pieces were all about. And it does explain a lot of things about Mom," she said. "It might explain why she was so strait-laced, and it almost certainly explains why she was so supportive of your artistic pursuits." I hadn't yet told Evelyn about my new career path. "It also explains *you*."

"What do you mean it explains *me*? What is it about me that needs explaining?"

"Well, I'm sure when I was born, Mom just gave in to Dad about naming me Evelyn." I must have looked puzzled. "It was Dad's grandmother's name. But when you came along, it sounds as if she had taken a bit more control of her life."

"I don't understand. What are you getting at?"

"You can be so dense sometimes, little sister. Why do you suppose she named you Charlotte?"

"Because she liked the name?"

"Think, Charlie. Because she was naming you after the lost love of her life. Charles. Chuck. You've been 'Charlie' from the moment Mom and Dad brought you home from the hospital. She always had a stronger connection to you than she did to me."

"I think I'm going to need something stronger than coffee." I got up and went to get the vodka and glasses from the cupboard.

"I'll just have another coffee," Evelyn said.

I almost got whiplash from turning toward her so fast. "What the..." Then I looked at her. And I knew what she wanted to talk to me about. "When –?"

"Is the baby due? Late in the summer."

"But I thought..."

"You thought that Michael didn't want children, and we were going to split up? Well, you know we did take a short break. Michael had something of a come-to-Jesus kind of moment while we were apart. He realized that the only reason he didn't want children was because he was scared. He is scared. I'm scared. Anyone who's having a baby ought to be scared. Anyway," she said, placing her hand on her still very flat stomach. "It happened, and we're over the moon." A slight cloud seemed to hover over her face for a moment. "But I'm only four weeks along. I haven't told a soul. You're the first one."

I was flattered. I got up, went around the table to pull her into a bear hug. "I'm going to be an aunt!" I honestly was excited.

"Now," she said, "Tell me all your news. When I walked in and saw you in that dress, I thought you'd been holding out on me about a man and a wedding."

It was time to tell her the rest of the story.

"Wow," she said when I'd finished telling her about Tom and moving in together. "And to think I'd flattered myself into thinking that he liked me when all along it was you." She peered at me closely. "So, are there wedding bells in the near future?"

"Whoa, slow down," I said. "We're only going to be sharing living space. And there's something else." I desperately needed to change the subject.

"I'm not sure I can handle any more news without a drink. So, you might have to wait until next fall to tell me whatever it is."

"I start a new job at the beginning of January."

It was as if I'd dropped a bomb. Evelyn's eyes just about popped out of her head, and she was, for once again, speechless. If I'd know these kinds of revelations were the way to make her stop talking, I'd have done it years ago.

"Details! I need details!" she said when she finally found her tongue once again.

So, I told her about the email from Princess Margaret College and the fact that I'd be moving in a new direction in my career. When I had finished, Evelyn was pensive.

"Are you sure about this?" This was not a question I expected to hear from Evelyn.

"Why do you ask? I thought you'd be cheering. It's not as if you haven't berated me for years about not having a 'real' job."

"I know, Charlie, but now it seems as if I might have been a teeny bit unfair to you."

Who is this woman, and what have you done with my sister? I had no idea where this was coming from.

"I might have been unfair to you and your writing talent," she continued. "I mean, if it's what you're supposed to do with your life, maybe you shouldn't be so cavalier about it. And as I've mentioned to you before, I have read your work. I think I may have read every single magazine piece you've ever published. You're actually good."

"You sound surprised. Anyway, I do have to make a living as well."

"But now that you have Tom..."

"Oh, so this is where this is coming from. If I have a man in my life – a man with money – I can rely on him. Evelyn Hudson, you are a hypocrite. You know that, don't you? That would be the last thing you'd ever want in your life."

She shrugged. "Sorry."

"Anyway, I said, "I love writing, and I'll always write. But I also love kids, and I love sharing my passion for writing with others. If I could inspire just a single student to write... Well, anyway, I've been thinking about something one of my MFA profs quoted to the class one time. '*Strive not to be a success, but rather to be of value.*'"

"Who in the world ever said that?" Ah, there was the old Evelyn emerging once again. All was right with the world.

"Just Albert Einstein."

"Well, there's nothing wrong with being a success, you know."

"I know that, Evelyn. But I think that I might be able to be both."

~

Evelyn stayed for two nights. When I told her that I'd have to pass on visiting her over the Christmas season, she really understood. Between packing and moving, not to mention preparing some classes to teach in January, I really couldn't get away. And, of course, then there was Tom. We had already made a date to hike into a Christmas tree farm to chop down a tree. This was going to be a very Christmassy Christmas this year. It would certainly be different from last year's season.

Evelyn had insisted on taking a photo of me wearing Mom's wedding dress – a wedding dress that had never been part of a wedding. I had a copy of the picture on my phone, and I thought Al might enjoy seeing it. I needed to thank him for all he'd done for me and make some plans for sewing in the new year. For that, I needed fabric.

When I rounded the corner into the street where *Sew Fine Things* had pride of place in the middle of the block, I was immediately confused. Was that a 'for sale' sign I could see on the building? Unaccountably, my heart started pounding so much so that I could hear it in my ears. I pushed open the door, and the little bell jangled as usual. I couldn't see Al, but that wasn't so unusual. He was often hidden among the ceiling-high shelves arranging bolts of fabric. I started looking at the new fabric arrivals when I heard a voice behind me.

"May I help you?" It was the same woman I'd met here before. She was wearing another brightly-coloured silk headscarf today. She seemed to recognize me. "Ah, you are Alvaro's friend." She walked behind the counter and pulled out an envelope from under the cash register. "Yes. You are Charlie Hudson." I nodded. "This is for you." She handed the envelope to me.

"Is Al here?"

"He is gone."

"Gone? Does this have something to do with the 'for sale' sign outside the building? Please tell me you're not closing."

She stood and folded her hands in front of her and smiled. "Alvaro has returned to where he belongs."

"To Syria?" I was horrified.

Al had told me he and his parents had immigrated to Canada soon after the civil war began. That was the only piece of personal information he ever shared with me. I had done some mental calculations at the time and figured that he must have been in his mid-twenties when he left Syria. I remembered being surprised that his English was perfect and almost non-accented.

She looked horrified. "Absolutely not! We are Canadians now. Syria is just the place we came from." She peered into my face. "We have never been properly introduced, have we?" I shook my head. She extended her hand. "I am Fatima Nassar." She shook my hand. "Alvaro's mother."

My hand stopped mid-shake. "I'm Charlotte Hudson."

"I am pleased to formally make your acquaintance, Charlotte Hudson. You did not know that I was Alvaro's mother, did you?"

"I didn't. He never said a thing about his family. Mrs. Nassar, if I may, where is Al then?"

Her smile was so broad I thought her face might split. Her eyes were shining. "As I said, he has returned to where he belongs. He begins his surgical residency in January."

"He's a doctor?" I was stunned. How could I have gotten to know someone over the course of almost a year and yet know absolutely nothing about him? Was I truly so self-centred that I didn't even register that others had lives as well?

"I am not surprised that he did not mention that he had graduated from medical school." She gestured toward the back of the store. "Charlotte, would you like to join me for a cup of coffee? I think Alvaro might like you to know him better."

And so, I followed her to a very pretty office that could not have been any more different from the organized chaos on the shop floor. The dove grey walls gave the space a soft, tranquil ambience. The centrepiece of the room was a large, blonde-wood desk where there was a computer on one end and bolts of fabric neatly stacked on the other end. The rest of the furniture was supple golden leather. The only bright pop of colour was the rug on the floor. I was staring at its intricate red and gold pattern as Mrs. Nassar made the coffee with a French press at a counter to the side.

She passed me a cup, then we sat on the leather couch. "I see you admiring the rug. It is one of the only things we brought with us from Damascus when we fled the regime and the terror. We were the lucky ones."

"Lucky?"

"We were lucky to come to Canada, where we have been able to make a life – and a nice living."

She then told me that Al's father had been a textile merchant with three thriving shops in Syria – two of which were in Damascus. They had been able to send their two children – Al and his younger sister – to private schools where they learned English. Al had also spent a semester at Oxford in England before being admitted to the medical school in Damascus. He had just graduated when the civil war began. They fled first to a refugee camp and then came to Canada, where Al's father was able to start a fabric business. Al helped in the shop like he'd been doing since he was thirteen.

"Alvaro had, of course, hoped that he could begin his medical residency, but it is difficult for foreign-trained doctors to find a placement. Alvaro helped his father build the business here. Then, when my husband died very unexpectedly four years ago, I could see that Alvaro was beginning to give up on his idea of ever pursuing his dream – of finishing what he had begun. He wanted to keep up the shop for me, but this is not right. We argued often. I could not let him give up his dream and his passion. I could not have lived with that. So, I helped him to study for the exams. In September, he travelled to Ottawa to write his exams. He is now in Montreal looking for an apartment so he can begin his residency. Finally, I am free as it turns out!"

And so, they were selling the building – which they owned – and the business, although Mrs. Nassar had no idea whether or not someone else would come along and continue it as a fabric store or renovate and start a new business. We heard the doorbell jangle, so Mrs. Nassar excused herself and left me to finish my second cup of coffee.

I was feeling oddly affected by her story. I was happy for Al, but I was also a bit forlorn. I felt as if I'd lost a friend. I hadn't realized how much I'd come to rely on Al's wisdom – and not just about fabrics and sewing. I felt the envelope that I'd stuck in my pocket. I tentatively pulled it out and looked at it. I slid my finger under the seal and tore it open.

Inside was a hand-written note from Al.

"*Dear Charlie. It has been my great privilege to have met you this year. I have watched you go from strength to strength not only in your sewing but also in your life. You have permitted me to help you, and you were a ray of sunshine each time you returned. For this I will be forever grateful.*" He was grateful? I was the one who should be thanking him. I read on. "*Since I have been in North America, I have read widely. I have even read the famous American writer Maya Angelou. It was she who said this: 'People will forget what you said; people will forget what you did, but people will never forget how you made them feel.' Charlie, I will never forget how you made me feel. Al.*"

Mrs. Nassar returned, carrying three bolts of fabric. "Charlotte, Al asked me to show these to you."

But I couldn't see them. Not through my tears.

~

My writing group had planned a festive celebration one week before Christmas. We were all to bring festive food and a piece of festive writing to read. I had most of the house packed up and ready to move – some of it to a recycler and the rest to come with me. I had been waxing so nostalgic to Tom about the red Formica kitchen table that he told me to bring it along. I had no idea what we'd do with it, but it was going to the house with me – as was Junior, of course.

I arrived at Miriam's that evening with a plate of shortbread cookies I'd picked up at one of my favourite bakeries. Everything in my kitchen was gone or packed. I hoped that they'd forgive me. I was the second last to arrive – Wendy would be along – and found the other three already toasting with eggnog laced with brandy, Joseph's specialty. You could see the whipped cream that he'd folded into it at the last minute. It was beyond decadent.

"Merry Christmas, Charlie," Karl said as he bear-hugged me.

"Happy holidays, Merry Christmas, Happy Hanukah..." Joseph liked to cover all the bases.

Even Miriam seemed jovial this evening. It turned out she'd been appointed poet-in-residence by the city library for the coming year. It was quite an accomplishment. I wondered what they'd think about my news about Princess Margaret College.

Wendy arrived, and we decided to approach the evening with a new twist: eat first, read later. When everyone else had done the eating and their reading, it was my turn.

"I don't have a written piece this evening," I said. "I want to tell you a story."

The story was about a young woman named Kat, who moved from small-town Canada to New York City to chase her dream of being a fashion designer. I told them about her fight with her parents, her excitement of being at the Parsons School, of hanging out with Janis Joplin at Woodstock, of planning a wedding, of losing her love to the Vietnam war, of giving up her dream of being an artist. When I had finished, I really felt as if the story resonated. It was where I had to start.

Miriam spoke first. "A captivating story, Charlie, but I'd lose that part about meeting Janis. Too unbelievable."

"Who's Janis Joplin?" Wendy said as she sipped her third eggnog. She licked the whipped cream from her upper lip.

Joseph, who was the font of pop-culture wisdom, rolled his eyes. "Look her up," he said, thrusting his phone into her hands.

Karl crossed his arms and looked at me. "Great story, Charlie. And the part about meeting Janis? Leave it in." He nodded at me. Somehow, he seemed to know.

"Kat gives up her dream in the story," I said, "but do you consider the change in her life's path to be selling out?" I looked around at my colleagues.

"Not necessarily," Joseph said. "Is this part of the story's theme?"

"Not really," I said, clearing my throat. "But it does resonate with me at this moment." I hesitated, hoping that they'd understand. "I've accepted a teaching job. I start in January."

There was a collective intake of breath.

"Well, well, well," Miriam said. "You know what they say. '*Those who can, do Those who can't, teach.*'"

"I think it's more properly, '*Those who can, do. Those who can do more, teach.*'" Karl was probably the only one in the room who truly got it.

"Well, I think it's lovely," Wendy said. "I think Charlie will make a terrific teacher. You know you *can* fit writing in with other things." She stared at Miriam. It was the first time I'd ever seen her stand up to Miriam. Bravo, Wendy!

Joseph hugged me. "You'll be a terrific teacher. The kids will love you, Charlie." Then a cloud flitted over his face. "But you'll never come back to the writing group, will you?"

"Why not?" I said. And at that moment, I knew that there was no need for me to leave everything behind to start something new. It wasn't my revolution – it was my evolution.

"I'll still be here," Karl said. Everyone else smiled and nodded in agreement.

And so, the writing group was given a new lease on life.

~

Sharing Christmas with Tom was as wonderful as I thought it would be. The enormous tree filled the front hall soaring two stories high. It had taken us two days to do all the decorating between Tom's work schedule and my moving activities. But when it was finished, it was magical. The hundreds of lights twinkled off the chandelier above it and gave the whole house a feeling of warmth and family. I hadn't completely moved in yet, but the house – with Tom – was beginning to feel like home.

By the end of the month, Mom's house was empty and clean, ready for its new family to move in on January 1. On the morning of December 31, I drove from Tom's – our – house by myself back to do one final check. I stood in the empty living room and gazed out the window at the snow covering the front lawn. This was the room where Evelyn and I had spent our own childhood Christmas mornings. It was also where Mom and Dad had taken our photos as we stood in front of the fireplace on any number of occasions – photos that included an assortment of prom dates through the years and Evelyn in her wedding gown with Dad before we all went to the church. There were lots of great memories here, but everything comes to an end. What I know for sure is that recognizing when something has come to an end is the only way for new beginnings to take shape. Even poet Henry Wadsworth Longfellow had an opinion on endings and beginnings when he wrote: *Great is the art of beginning, but greater is the art of ending.* I knew I was in good company.

December 31 (one year later)

"Charlie! Charlie! What in the world are you doing in there?" Evelyn was banging on the door of the bathroom in the hotel suite she and I were sharing. "Do you know what time it is?"

I actually did know what time it was. I was sitting on the closed top of the toilet, trying to have a single moment of peace before all hell broke loose. And with Evelyn, we were always just this close to that edge.

"Charlie!" The pounding started again. "Come out here this minute!"

It was no use. My moment was over. I stood up and looked at myself in the mirror. I looked pretty damn good, even if I did say so myself. I was wearing a touch of makeup, and my hair in its loose bun was looking sophisticated. "Mom," I said to the mirror, "I hope you're up there watching." And I blew her a kiss across the ether. It was time. Evelyn would not be put off any longer.

When I emerged from the bathroom, Evelyn was standing there holding the dress. "Get over here. Tom won't wait forever."

"I think he just might," I said, teasing her. Evelyn was so consumed by details she was easy to tease.

I stepped into the dress and pulled it up. She zipped it up and stood back. "Here. Put on your shoes."

I did as I was told then stepped in front of the full-length mirror on its stand in the corner. We both gasped. Staring back at both of us was Mom's doppelganger, but it was me. Just me.

"Charlie, you look beautiful." This was a far cry from her reaction to the first dress I'd made from that hideous shower curtain. But she was right. I did look beautiful. I finally had somewhere to wear Mom's lace dress that I'd finished.

The dress had hung in the back of the walk-in closet I shared with Tom ever since I'd moved in a year ago. One day in June, Tom had come downstairs holding the dress. I remembered being alarmed that he'd found it. I hoped he didn't think I had it there for any other reason than it had been my mother's.

"Charlie, I found this dress in your closet."

"I think I told you about Mom's dress. That's it."

"Well, great," he had said, putting it down on the arm of the chair where I was reading a book. "Because I think it will go beautifully with this." And he handed me a small turquoise box. From Tiffany's. Of course, I said yes.

Now here we were. Evelyn had taken over the wedding planning the minute she had recovered from giving birth at the end of August to baby Katherine (not to be called Kat, Evelyn told me in no uncertain terms). The recovery had taken little more than a week, and she was off on wedding planning, little Katherine in tow. Michael and Katherine were now in the hotel room next door while Evelyn and I had stayed the night before the wedding in the honeymoon suite as it was quaintly called.

"We have half an hour before we have to be downstairs, Evelyn. Let's have a glass of champagne before the final prep."

She looked at the bottle of *Veuve Clicquot* cooling in the silver ice bucket. It was a gift from Tom, and it just happened to be her favourite champagne as well. She expertly popped the cork and poured two flutes. "Here's to..." Evelyn stopped as she spied something on the table. "What's that?"

I picked the book up off the table and gave it to her. The cover said, "*Kat's Kosmic Blues. A novel. By C .K. Hudson.*"

"You said that wasn't due out until the spring!" Evelyn was almost shouting with glee. "It's an advance copy!"

"Yup," I said. "And it's for you."

She put her flute down and hugged me. Then she picked up the glass again and lifted it for a toast. "To C. K. Hudson. May she always write her truth."

I was hoping a story about a young woman named Kat, who moved from small-town Canada to New York City to chase her dream of being a fashion designer...well, you know the rest... might be something others might enjoy. My new agent thought so. So did the publisher who bought it. They even let me leave in the part about when Kat meets Janis Joplin.

It is never too late to be what you might have been. ~ George Elliot

About the Author

Patricia J. Parsons (aka P J Parsons) has written a dozen books, including health and business books, as well as a memoir and two historical novels in addition to her women's fiction. She has been a fashion design and sewing fanatic for most of her life, a passion she writes about online at *The GG Files blog*. She lives, writes and sews in Toronto.

Connect with her on Instagram @patriciajparsons

Join her on Facebook @patriciaparsonswriter

Visit her web site at www.patriciajparsons.com

Some other books by Patricia J. Parsons

Plan B (lit-for-intelligent-chicks)

Confessions of a Failed Yuppie (lit-for-intelligent-chicks)

Something More Than Love (historical fiction)

Grace Note: In Hildegard's Shadow (historical fiction)

Another 'Pointe' of View: The Life & Times of a Ballet Mom (memoir)

KAT'S KOSMIC BLUES

C. K. Hudson

"No daughter of mine is going to an art college!" My father crumpled my acceptance letter from the Nova Scotia College of Art and Design, which I had only a moment ago shared so proudly with him and threw it into the wastebasket in his den. "You'll accept the offer from the University of Toronto and study to become a teacher like any proper young woman should do." His face was red, his eyes bulging. I wished, ever so briefly, that he'd die. Right this moment. Right there in front of me. But he didn't.

It was 1965. I was nineteen years old and didn't consider myself to be proper. And I was angrier than I had ever been in my life. I was still outraged three months later, when I unpacked my suitcases and settled into my residence room at Ardmore Hall in Toronto. At least I was more than 1000 miles away from my father.

...coming in 2021...

Kat's story

www.ingramcontent.com/pod-product-compliance
Lightning Source LLC
Chambersburg PA
CBHW030547310726
48979CB00010B/2068/J

* 9 7 8 1 7 7 7 2 4 3 1 1 1 *